EMLYN'S MOON

'The blue door opened and Nia was pitched into
Wonderland. Astonished and enchanted, she
forgot her fear and murmured . . .

From floor to ceiling the walls of the chapel had
been covered with bright paintings. Patterns of
trees and fields jostled with fantastic flowers, with
faces that Nia knew, and some that she did not.'

JENNY NIMMO

Emlyn's Moon

Illustrated by Joanna Carey

MAMMOTH

First published 1987
by Methuen Children's Books Ltd
Magnet edition published 1988
Reissued 1989 by Mammoth
Reprinted 1990
an imprint of Mandarin Paperbacks
Michelin House, 81 Fulham Road, London SW3 6RB

Text copyright © 1987 Jenny Nimmo
Illustrations copyright © 1987 Joanna Carey

ISBN 0 7497 0703 8

Printed in Great Britain
by Cox & Wyman Ltd, Reading

For my mother

CONTENTS

EMLYN'S MOON

1
The Boy from the Chapel

'Don't go into Llewelyn's chapel!' they told Nia. 'No good will come of it. Something happened there!' But Nia disobeyed. If she hadn't, nothing would have changed. She'd still be plain Nia, dull Nia, Nia who couldn't do anything!

It all began on the day they left Tŷ Llŷr. The children, tucked between boxes in the back of the Landrover, were waiting for their mother to lock up. Nia was propped on a rolled mattress at the open end of the car. She was gazing at a red geranium in the kitchen window, the only bright thing left. And then the flower was lifted out of the dark window by unseen hands. It reappeared in the doorway, perched upon a pile of towels in her mother's arms.

'I nearly forgot it!' Mrs Lloyd beamed over the geranium.

Nia wished she *had* forgotten the flower; just for a day or two. At least there would have been something left alive in Tŷ Llŷr. If a house could look forlorn, then that's how Tŷ Llŷr seemed to her: curtains gone from the windows, the farmyard bare and tidy, and a stillness so unnatural it almost hurt. A stray feather drifted in the sunlight, the

11

only reminder that chickens had once inhabited the yard. It was May but the ewes and their lambs had gone, and the only sounds came from bees in the giant sycamore tree.

Even the children in the Landrover were silent. Leaving their home had ceased to be an exciting idea; suddenly it had become a rather shocking reality.

Mrs Lloyd climbed up to sit beside her husband. The engine started. The spell was broken. An excited shouting and chattering broke out.

Nia was the only one to look back and see the boy beneath the sycamore. He was standing so close to the shadowy tree-trunk that she could barely make out his shape. But she knew it was Gwyn Griffiths by the mass of dark hair and the way he stood, hands in pockets, so very still and thoughtful. No other boy could do that.

Nia nudged her brother, wedged in beside her. 'Look, Alun! There's Gwyn!'

There was so much noise, so much movement amongst the seven children packed tightly together between boxes and cases, that Alun neither felt nor heard Nia, so she raised her own hand and waved, rather tentatively.

The boy beneath the tree responded.

'He's waving, Alun!' Nia shouted above the rumpus.

'What? Who?'

'Gwyn!'

'Oh!'

'He's come to say ''goodbye'', Alun! Quick!'

Alun leant over his sister, accidentally knocking the sheep-dog's nose with his elbow. Fly yelped, the Landrover lurched round a bend and Alun was flung backwards on top of his twin brothers. Siôn and Gareth were too happy to grumble.

Gwyn Griffiths disappeared from sight.

The Landrover rattled on, down the mountain, gathering speed as the lane became steeper, and the chatter in the back increased to an hysterical crescendo of excitement; Catrin even broke into song.

Mr Lloyd joined in, humming gustily. He'd done it at last; broken free of the farm that his ailing father-in-law had begged him to take over. Iestyn Lloyd was a small, dark man, his face as weather-tanned as any hill-farmer, but he was too fond of his food and a good pint to stay as fit as he should, too gregarious to enjoy the solitary existence that suited his neighbour, Ivor Griffiths, so well. But he had tried, no one could say he hadn't. For fifteen years he'd struggled with hard mountain earth, with ewes trapped in snow and lambs lost, and he had failed. He would never make a good farmer, his heart wasn't in it, and with another child on the way, he had to find some way of earning a decent living. When the butcher's shop in Pendewi came up for sale, it was like an answer to Iestyn's prayers. He'd been an apprentice butcher, it was what he knew, what he could do best. He would succeed this time. He'd sold his stock and all his land to Ivor Griffiths, who had a magic touch when it came to animals, and a way of knowing the land that only a born farmer could have.

No one wanted the farmhouse though. No one wanted ancient Tŷ Llŷr, with its crumbling chimney, its family of bats, and the plum trees that curled their way under the wavy roof.

'Mae hen wlad fy nhadau yn annwyl i mi,' sang Mr Lloyd, breaking out in a rare exhibition of patriotism, as he cheerfully sped away from the things that Nia loved.

Fly, the sheep-dog, rolled her eyes and gazed imploringly at Nia. The dog, at least, felt as apprehensive as she.

There was nothing in Pendewi for Nia. She had neither the talents nor the aspirations of her brothers and sisters. In Pendewi there was a library for Nerys to browse in every day, if she wished. For Catrin, a music teacher only two doors away, and a disco on Saturdays. For the boys, shops stuffed with comics and bubblegum, with batteries and nails, glue and string. There they would all be, crammed into their little rooms above the shop, reading and singing, building, hammering and chewing, while the plums turned from green to gold in the orchard at Tŷ Llŷr, and strangers put them into baskets and carried them away.

No one would notice the wild Welsh poppies that Nia had nurtured in little places by the stream, or see the white roses behind the farmhouse. The garden would become a carpet of petals and then, when the wind came, the petals would scatter over the mountain like snow. And no one seemed to care, not even Mrs Lloyd, preoccupied as she was with thoughts of the baby who would come in summer, when the plums were turning gold.

Gwyn Griffiths' sister had loved flowers, but she had vanished on the mountain, no one knew how.

'I wish you had waved to Gwyn!' Nia said to Alun, but she spoke half to herself, and did not expect him to hear.

The Landrover slowed down before turning into the main road. Summer visitors had begun to arrive and the road was busy. Mr Lloyd swung in behind a caravan, and there they stayed, unable to pass the clumsy vehicle, and travelling so slowly that Nia could count the primroses on the verge.

At the top of the hill leading down into Pendewi, the caravan stopped without warning. Mr Lloyd jammed on his brakes and leant out of the window, mouthing oaths

14

about visitors and caravans; he could see the owner in the driving seat of his smart red car, unconcernedly reading a map. Mr Lloyd banged his fist on the horn. The children pressed forward, anticipating a row, all except for Nia, who had noticed something far more interesting.

The Landrover had stopped beside the old chapel; the chapel that wasn't a chapel now, but a home for someone. The gate and the iron railings had been painted pink and gold; the door was blue with big golden flowers on it and bright curtains framed the long windows. When Nia stood up she could see down into the room beyond the window. A boy in green trousers lay sprawled across a rug; he was doing something with his hands, making something, but Nia couldn't see what it was. Curious, she leant further out, but as she did so the Landrover suddenly jerked forward. Nia screamed and clutched wildly at the air, trying to keep her balance.

The boy in the chapel looked up in surprise, and then grinned at Nia's predicament, before Alun caught the back of her jersey and pulled her to safety.

'What on earth were you doing?' Nerys, the eldest, inquired tetchily. She felt responsible for incidents in the back of the Landrover.

'I was just looking,' Nia replied.

'Looking at what?'

'Just into the chapel. I saw Emlyn Llewelyn from school. I didn't know he lived there!'

'Course he does,' said Alun. 'Him and his dad. It's a bad place that!'

'Who says?'

'Gwyn says!'

'Why?'

'Something happened there, didn't it?' Alun said

15

world-wearily.

'What happened?' Nia persisted.

'I donno; something bad! It's all wrong that place. No one goes there!'

'It's beautiful!' Nia protested. 'And I like Emlyn.'

'You don't know, do you?' Alun said in a grim and rather condescending manner.

Nia was silent. Why had she defended Emlyn? She hardly knew him. He was in Alun's class and nearly two years older than herself. She wished she had been able to see further into his strange home.

Outside Pendewi the caravan turned left on to the sea road, and the Landrover continued on, down into the little market town.

Sunshine flooded the High Street. The trees were in blossom and Saturday shoppers in bright spring clothes, bustled in and out of the narrow grey-tiled houses. It wasn't such a bad place after all, Nia thought.

The Lloyds parked outside a tall black and white building at the furthest end of the town. There was a huge blue van in front of them, with removal men in grey overalls munching sandwiches in the cabin. The furniture was all in place.

There were two entrances; one that led into a shop furbished with red carcases and neat trays of sliced meat; the other, a very private-looking black door with a brass number 6 on it.

The family went into their new home through the black and private door, leaving it open to allow warmth and light into the dark house.

Mr Lloyd persuaded the reluctant and grumbling Fly down a long passage to the back garden. Mrs Lloyd sank into a sunny chair by the door; she was still carrying the red geranium.

The four boys clattered noisily up the stairs and along the creaking and uncarpeted landing, eager to break into boxes that had been withheld for weeks; to find ancient and beloved toys and strew them across floorboards of unfamiliar rooms and make them theirs, their fortress and their home.

Nerys, Nia and Catrin stood before their mother, flushed and still pretty in her flowery smock.

'Well, I think it's upstairs first, girls. When the clothes are in the drawers and the beds are made, we'll have a cup of tea.'

Nia followed her older sisters upstairs. Nerys and Catrin disappeared into a room overlooking the High Street. Nia glimpsed a wide sunlit window before the door was closed against her.

Opposite her sisters' room, Siôn, Gareth and Alun had already extended their territory. A wooden railway track snaked through their open door, and along the landing. Nia side-stepped, too late! She tripped and a red engine flew across the floor.

'Watch it!' the twins sang out. 'Nia-can't-do-nothing! Nia-in-the-middle! Nia's got a funny tooth, and her nose goes squiggle, squiggle!'

Nia was fed up with the twins' new rhyme, but she couldn't think of a suitably clever retort. It was all true, of course, that was the worst of it. They'd got her, pinned her down like a butterfly on a board, only she was more of a moth; a very ordinary brown moth who wasn't good at anything except screwing up her nose when she didn't understand. A moth in the middle; with two butterfly sisters and an older brother who could mend anything; with two younger brothers who could stand on their heads,

17

and an even younger one who got by just because he was the youngest, and had curls.

She retrieved the red engine and put it into Siôn's hand. 'It's Iolo's engine, anyway,' she said.

The twins allowed Nia to escape without further aggravation. She continued down the corridor until she reached two open doors at the end. To her left, the bathroom, bright with sunlight and frosted glass. Iolo was playing with something in the basin; little waves of soapy water were spilling over on to the floor.

Let someone else find the puddle! Leaving Iolo in peace Nia turned to the room on her right; the room she was to share with Iolo. There were no spaces left for her in her sisters' room and none for Iolo in his brothers'. They would have to put up with each other for the time being. As they had grown in size and number, the Lloyd children had become used to an annual re-arrangen.ent of bedrooms. If the new baby was a girl, Nia would share her bright little room at the top of the house, if not, Iolo would move in with the new brother and Nia would stay here, in this small, shadowy room, that had an old and unused air about it.

The window looked out on to the back garden, a garden in shadow with hardly a blade of grass. There was the river to look at though, splashing over bleached pebbles beyond the garden wall. And, on the other side of the river, Morgan-the-Smithy's long black barn with blue sparks lighting the windows, and Morgan and his sons singing in green boilersuits

Next year there would be flowers growing by the river. Nia fumbled in her pockets and brought out a tiny paper parcel. She carefully unfolded the paper and laid on the floor a part of Tŷ Llŷr: honesty seeds in their flat, silvery shells, tiny black poppy and campion seeds, all mixed together, so that when she sowed them next spring, the meagre little patch below would be splashed with orange and purple and pink.

'What's that?' Iolo had finished with boats and stood dripping in the doorway.

'Seeds,' Nia replied. 'You'd better dry yourself and the floor, or you'll get a row.'

'I can't find a towel,' Iolo explained.

Nia could hear her mother moving about in the room above them. 'I'll look downstairs for you; Mam had them in the hall.'

'I need something to eat too,' Iolo informed her.

'I'll see.'

Nia tucked her precious seeds back into a pocket and went downstairs.

Sunlight was streaming through a semi-circle of stained-glass above the front door. The hall was lined with a clutter of cases, bags and upturned chairs, but in the centre there was only one thing; a box, *the* box! Nia recognised it; it contained Mam's clothes from twenty years before; dresses that were too tight, but too full of memories to throw away; shoes too flimsy, beads too bright for a mother of seven. It was like a gift, wrapped in the glowing colours from the stained-glass window. A gift for Nia-can't-do-nothing, who could now become Nia-can-do-anything!

Forgetting Iolo and towels, Nia knelt beside the box and began to pick at the string that held it shut. The string fell off and she opened the box. Almost reverently she began to lift out the contents and lay them on the floor.

There were shouts from above and around Nia but, amazingly, no one came into the hall. Catrin had found

19

the piano and was practising her scales. Fly was whining somewhere.

'Someone take the dog out!' Mr Lloyd shouted from the shop.

No one answered.

Nia had found a violet dress, patterned with pink and white flowers. She stood up and slipped it over her head. The hem touched the ground. She knelt again and scrabbled in the box, trying to find the thing she needed. There it was – a wide-brimmed red straw hat. And now she could feel the little paper bundles of beads and shoes at the bottom of the box. She drew out a rope of big silver shells and a pair of pink shoes with stars on them.

Nia kicked off her trainers and stepped into the pink shoes; the violet dress covered them; she would trip. The silver shells would have to become a belt. They encircled her waist perfectly, not a shell too long. Nia hitched the dress a few inches over the shell-belt, just enough to reveal the shoes. She was almost ready.

The finishing touch was a long string of multi-coloured beads wound once, twice, three times round her neck.

Catrin moved on from Mendelssohn to Mozart and Fly's distant whine became a long, low howl.

'Someone take that poor dog for a walk,' Mrs Lloyd pleaded from a box-lined room upstairs.

'I'll go,' answered Nia.

'Don't let her off the lead; she's not used to the town,' came a voice muffled by mounds of linen. 'And don't go into any shops.'

'I won't!'

'Poor thing! She can't stay here much longer.' The rest of Mrs Lloyd's words were drowned by Fly's howl of agreement.

Nia tottered down the passage and opened the back door. Four stone steps led down into the yard. Fly was tied to the rail beside the steps, with just enough lead to allow her to stretch out, head on paws, in a tiny patch of sunlight that had managed to creep round the house. The dog leapt up when she saw Nia, and barked joyfully.

'Sssh!' Nia knew her father would not approve of her outfit if he saw her. She began to untie Fly's lead, all the while eyeing the long room that extended into the yard beyond the rest of the house; the hateful room that held all those dead and dreadful things. Through the tiny window she glimpsed a red carcase, swinging where her father had just hung it. Mr Lloyd was whistling; happy among his sides of beef, his lamb chops and purple pigs' livers. Poor dead, dismembered creatures. It was enough to put you off meat forever.

'Ugh!' Nia could even smell them.

Fly, free at last, bounded up the steps, dragging Nia behind her. They flew down the passage and through the hall, Fly scattering discarded cardboard and all the rubbish of removal, Nia sliding and tripping in the outsize

21

pink shoes.

Nerys appeared at the top of the stairs, alerted by the commotion. 'Nia, what are you . . . ?'

But Nia had opened the front door and leapt through it before her sister had time to take in her appearance.

Fly began to live up to her name; her paws barely touched the ground as she tore joyfully up the street.

The pink shoes hadn't a chance; first one flew off and then the other. Nia dared not stop to retrieve them for fear of choking Fly. Clasping the red hat to her head with her free hand, she careered after the dog, darting between startled shoppers and shouts of 'Watch it!', 'Mind the pram!', 'Where are you going, girl?', 'Good God, what's she doing?'.

Not a very favourable first appearance, Nia thought.

Fly bounded on, back towards Tŷ Llŷr and the mountain fields. The road became steeper and, at the end of the town, the dog stopped and stared mournfully up the hill, her sides heaving and her long tongue hanging out like a wet flag.

Nia dropped down beside Fly, in worse shape than the dog. They sat side by side on the hot paving stones, gasping and panting. Nia felt as though she'd spent a month in the desert. She closed her eyes and leant against Fly's woolly neck. When she opened them again a few moments later, she found herself looking at a shop window, and at a boy moving past the window and into the shop; he was a tall boy with thick brown-gold hair and green trousers – the boy from the chapel.

Afterwards, Nia could never remember whether it was thirst or curiosity that lead her to follow him. Whatever it was, she forgot all the rules, all the warnings about sheepdogs in shops, and followed Emlyn Llewelyn through the

door.

The wide back of a woman in brown obliterated most of the counter. The wide woman was whispering to the shopkeeper, a man in red braces and a grubby shirt, who seemed more interested in gossip than business. Nia had time to contemplate the rows of sweets and biscuits before making a decision. She spied cans of fruit juice on the highest shelf. On the other side of the shop, Emlyn Llewelyn was bending over tubes of glue.

'Yes?' The shopkeeper was staring suspiciously at Nia.

The wide woman had rolled back, propping herself up on the counter; she was staring at Nia's bare feet.

Nia tried to smile but instead screwed up her nose.

'I want a drink, please!' she said quickly.

'Get what you want then. Can you reach?'

'I think so.' Nervous of the disapproving glances Nia thoughtlessly let the loop of Fly's lead slip down her arm, and reached for a can of orange juice. Just as her fingertips touched the can, two more customers entered the shop. Fly panicked; she leapt away from the shelves growling anxiously. Nia was jerked backwards, her heel caught in the hem of the violet dress and she tumbled to the floor, followed by a pile of cans. Suddenly the whole top shelf became possessed. Cans and bottles tottered and clinked and began to roll towards her. There was nothing Nia could do to halt that dreadful and inexorable shower of cans. Some fell on top of her, some crashed to the ground and others were caught by a darting figure in green trousers. She was aware of the shopkeeper hopping up and down beside her, kicking out at the barking Fly and screaming, 'Who's going to pay? Look at the shop!' and low voices murmuring, 'It shouldn't be allowed!', 'She's no shoes!', 'And look at the hat!', 'What's her mam

24

thinking of?', 'Get the dog out!', 'No shoes! No shoes!'.

And then a boy's voice said, 'It isn't a crime, having no shoes!' and Emlyn Llewelyn stepped forward, holding Fly tight by the collar. 'Only two cans are damaged,' he said, 'and we'll buy those. Come on!' He tapped Nia on the shoulder and held out his free hand.

Nia looked up. Emlyn had never spoken to her before; he had golden eyes, like a lion.

'Come on!' commanded Emlyn Llewelyn.

Nia put her hand in his and he helped her to her feet.

'You'd better hold your dog,' he said, 'and pull your dress up or you'll trip again.'

Nia obeyed and Emlyn placed a pile of coins on the counter. Then he strode out of the shop, dragging Nia with him.

'I owe you for the drink,' said Nia when the door had been closed against reproachful mutterings.

'That's OK!' Emlyn said. 'Are you all right?'

'Yes,' Nia lied. Her shins ached where the cans had hit them. 'But I'm thirsty.'

'Have it on me,' Emlyn held out a can. 'Dog looks thirsty too. It's a nice dog. What's its name?'

'Fly,' Nia replied, 'and it's a she.' She opened the can and tipped it to her lips, gulping and coughing as the fizzy drink trickled down her throat.

Emlyn watched her for a moment, politely refraining from mentioning the splutters, then he asked, 'Why don't you bring Fly up to my place and give her a drink?'

'I don't think I'd better,' Nia said. 'I must find Mam's shoes. They fell off when I was running, and they've got stars on them.'

'OK!' Emlyn accepted her refusal almost too fast, as though he expected it. He kicked the ground with the heel

25

of his sandal and looked away from her.

And suddenly Nia remembered what Alun had said about the chapel. 'Nobody goes there – something happened – it's no good!' and she suddenly found herself saying, 'All right! I'll come, just for a bit!'

She could see that Emlyn was more than pleased, but trying hard not to show it. 'Good!' he said. 'Can I take the dog?'

Nia handed him Fly's lead. 'I wanted to see inside your place,' she said.

Emlyn grinned. 'I thought I recognised you, spying on us. You're Alun's sister, aren't you? You look different in all that stuff. I wasn't sure.'

Nia giggled. 'I nearly fell out, didn't I?'

'What's going on? How is it you're in jeans one minute and then beads and a funny hat?'

'We've moved,' said Nia. ' ''Moved with the times!'' That's what my dad says.'

They began to walk up the hill. Fly too hot and thirsty now to run, and Emlyn striding out faster than the dog. Nia had to take little running-hopping steps in order to keep up with the boy and to avoid loose stones on the ground.

Once a van passed on the other side of the road, its engine coughing as it strained up the hill, and Fly rushed at it barking furiously, just as she used to do when strangers passed Tŷ Llŷr.

'She doesn't like cars and that sort of thing,' Nia explained breathlessly. 'She wants to go home, like me. Only it isn't home any more; the farm, I mean, where we come from.'

'Where did you come from?'

'Tŷ Llŷr, on the mountain. Dad didn't like it, the work

was too rough; sheep kept dying and that in the winter, and Mam said the house was too small with another baby coming, but you'd have thought she'd want to stay, being as it was her home all her life, she was even born there. Nobody wanted to stay except me and Fly. I planted flowers there, see. I like to watch things grow and all the colours.'

'Are there a lot of you?' Emlyn inquired. He was gazing intently at Fly and, for a moment, Nia wondered if he really wanted an answer.

'Seven!' she replied. 'Seven children, that is, and I'm in the middle, right in the very middle. Nerys is the oldest, she's clever and quite pretty, but Catrin is beautiful. She called herself Kate last year, she thought it sounded more romantic but now she's Catrin again; she plays the piano and her hair is – oh . . . ' Nia sighed, 'all pale yellow and floating, like . . . like ash trees.'

Emlyn looked at her with interest but he said nothing and Nia began to wonder if she'd talked too much. She'd never been able to express herself before and couldn't think how it had come about. They walked on in silence until they reached the pink and gold railings of the chapel and all at once Nia began to feel afraid. Fly was apprehensive too; she kept making worried rumbling noises in her throat.

It was too bright: the painted door, the coloured curtains; it was like the house of gingerbread that had tempted Hansel and Gretel, and look what had become of them! 'Something happened in that place, something bad . . . ' Alun's words kept repeating themselves in her head, but Emlyn had taken her hand and was drawing her up the steps to the door!

2
A
Promise
– Broken

The blue door opened and Nia was pitched into Wonderland. Astonished and enchanted, she forgot her fear and murmured, 'Oh! I didn't know! I didn't know!'

From floor to ceiling the walls of the chapel had been covered with bright paintings. Patterns of trees and fields jostled with fantastic flowers, with faces that Nia knew, and some that she did not. Coloured birds swooped through clouds and rainbows and a boy with gold-brown hair tumbled in the corn, swung from green branches and slept beside a stream.

'I can see you,' said Nia quietly. 'You and your life. Who did it?'

'My dad,' said Emlyn, not proud, but pleased that she was impressed.

Above her, huge coloured butterflies floated on glittering threads from the vaulted ceiling, and all about the room wonderful wooden beasts gazed out with brilliant painted eyes.

'And did he make these?' Nia nodded at the beasts and the butterflies.

'All of it!' Emlyn closed the door. The butterflies shivered in the draught and the whole ceiling spun and shone.

Was this why everyone avoided the chapel? Just because it was extraordinary. There were no demons here.

Sunlight, pouring through the long windows, dazzled Nia and she dared not move for fear of stumbling on a treasure. Something large and dark stooped at the far end of the chapel, but she could not make out what kind of creature it was for its outline was blurred against the glare. And then it began to move. It rose and rose until its long shadow almost touched her feet.

A tall man in a black boiler suit was approaching; his hair a lion's mane, his eyes golden, like Emlyn's. A large hand clasped Nia's and a deep voice asked, in Welsh, 'Beth ydi'ch enw chi?'

'Her name is Nia,' Emlyn answered for the speechless girl, 'and her dog wants a drink!'

'Dog?' Mr Llewelyn dropped Nia's hand and regarded the bewildered Fly peering round Emlyn's legs. 'Good God, boy! I told you not to bring dogs in here. He'll wreck my work!'

'I'll take it out, Dad. And it's a *she*; her name is Fly.'

'Fly, is it? Well, remove Fly and give her a drink from the trough.'

'And can I let her loose in the field, Dad?'

'Ask the lady,' boomed Mr Llewelyn. 'It's her dog.'

Nia nodded.

'Let the dog loose, Emlyn boy. And I will entertain your visitor. Here, lady, have a seat!'

Abandoned by the boy and the dog, Nia perched uncertainly on the edge of the cane chair that Emlyn's father drew out for her.

'And now, before tea,' Idris Llewelyn's dark presence loomed over Nia, 'may I make a small sketch of you, Nia?

29

So splendid in your beads, and with silver shells all round your waist! And, ah, what a hat!'

Nia had a great desire to break out of the cane chair, but she could not. There was something reassuring about the kindly wooden beasts, the painted landscapes and the bright butterfly ceiling. So she curled herself tighter into the chair, while Mr Llewelyn pulled a stool beneath the north window and took up a large sketch pad.

Cocooned in soft cushions, Nia relaxed and let her eyes explore the chapel. In a corner by the door she noticed a truckle bed covered with a striped blanket; Emlyn's place, she decided. There were piles of books under the bed and, beside it, small wooden animals, some perfect and some whose heads and legs were still encased in uncarved blocks of wood. There were empty tubes of glue, pieces of string, scraps of paper, a penknife and a magnifying glass, but no Lego, no model cars, not a toy of any sort.

At the other end of the chapel a huge brass bedstead protruded from behind a wicker screen. It was an ancient bed with wonderful knobs and decorations, some scratched and some repainted; its satin cover was patterned with splashes of red and green and gold, the sort of transport you would need for a very special dream. And then Nia noticed something that made her fingers tighten. Her tiny intake of breath caused Mr Llewelyn to glance at her face but he said nothing.

Nia quickly looked away from the thing that had disturbed her, but when the artist looked back at his work, she found herself gazing at the bed again. The hem of the beautiful bedcover was scarred by a long black mark. Some of the coloured threads had been severed at the edge, and hung in uneven sooty strands. It was a small thing but ugly and, somehow, alarming.

30

She decided to count the piles of rugs that were scattered on the bare floorboards, each one a different size, a different colour.

Mr Llewelyn, a pencil in his mouth, smiled and said, 'We've been wanderers, you see. Our collection was gathered from every part of the world, but now we must stay put while Emlyn goes to school.'

'And will you go away again, when Emlyn has grown?' Nia asked.

Mr Llewelyn was silent for a while, dabbing at his sketchbook, and then he muttered, almost to himself, 'Perhaps . . . one day . . . '

Emlyn came in and placed a kettle on a rusty gas stove in a corner. There was an ancient sink beside the stove, with cupboards above and below it. A teapot appeared, and three blue mugs. Everything you could need in one room, Nia thought. Just as it should be.

'Can we take the tea outside, Da, to keep Fly company?' Emlyn asked.

'Why not?' said Mr Llewelyn. He closed his sketchbook and put it on a table beside him. 'I'm not showing you yourself yet, Lady-with-the-Violet-Dress, because it's not finished. And you must come again, with your hat and your beads.'

'I could wear Mam's shoes,' said Nia eagerly, 'they've got stars on them.'

'Why not? Why not?' Mr Llewelyn laughed, very deep and loud, and helped her out of the chair.

They all went outside and sipped their tea at the back of the chapel, where a steep field of wild flowers stretched down and down to the river.

'Oh!' cried Nia joyfully. 'You can see the mountain from here; you could see Tŷ Llŷr too, if it wasn't for the

31

trees.'

'Ah, that mountain,' murmured Mr Llewelyn. 'You know Tŷ Bryn and Emlyn's cousin then?'

'Cousin?' Nia repeated, turning to Emlyn. 'Whose cousin are you?'

Emlyn did not reply. He picked up a stick and threw it for Fly.

'Gwyn Griffiths is his cousin,' said Mr Llewelyn. 'Their mothers were sisters, but you wouldn't know it. We're down here, and they're on the mountain, and there's a world between us.'

They all turned to look at the mountain as he spoke, and in that very second an extraordinary thing happened. A huge, shining cloud appeared from nowhere, right above the mountain and although the sun still shone, everything went very, very cold, and an icy gust blew Nia's hat on to the grass.

No one referred to the cloud, they just watched it, settling slowly on to the mountain. Emlyn went to fetch a tin of biscuits. They ate them all except one which they gave to Fly, who had begun to whine. And Nia became aware that hours, not minutes had passed. The sun was low, there were shoes to find, explanations to make up. She jumped up, rubbing her cold arms and crying, 'I must go. I'll get a row!'

'I'll come with you,' said Emlyn, grabbing Fly's collar.

'Yes, go with her, boy! And don't forget the hat.' Mr Llewelyn squashed the big hat down over Nia's ears and led them round to the front of the chapel.

As the children passed through the pink and gold gate, Mr Llewelyn exclaimed, 'By heck, it's cold. What's happened?'

'It's like a spell,' said Emlyn, laughing. 'Let's run

33

before we turn to stone.'

They scampered down the hill, Fly bounding beside them, forgetting where she was going, just happy to be running, and Emlyn shouted, breathless, 'Would your dad sell Fly to me? If I could get the money?'

'Don't know!' Nia called back. 'She's a sheep-dog, see, and valuable they say. My dad wants £30 at least. We can't keep her, that's sure. Anyway, what about your dad?'

'I can talk him round. I know I can!'

'Oooow!' Nia's bare toes had met something sharp and painful. She sat on the grass and examined her foot. It was extremely dirty but there was no blood to be seen.

'You all right?' Emlyn crouched beside her.

Fly began to bark.

'No blood,' said Nia. 'But I think I'll walk now and let the spell get me, if it can.'

They sauntered on until they reached the shop where it had all begun. It was closed and the street was empty. Emlyn said, 'I won't come any further. They might not like it, your mam and dad!'

'Why not?'

'Because they're from the mountain.'

'So?'

'I'll tell you one day.'

'What were you doing when I looked into the chapel?'

'Making an animal,' Emlyn grinned. 'That's why I came to the shop, for glue; the tail broke off.'

'What sort of animal?'

'It doesn't matter, just an animal. About the dog. I've got some money saved and I think Dad'll lend me the rest. I'll let you know at school on Monday. Promise not to let them sell Fly till then!'

34

'I promise,' said Nia, never dreaming that she could break her promise.

'Thanks!' Emlyn passed Fly's lead to her and turned to go.

'Emlyn?' Nia had remembered something that had been worrying her. 'Where's your mam?'

He stopped and stood quite still with his back to her. Nia thought he wasn't going to reply and wished she hadn't asked the question.

But Emlyn turned and, looking past her at the distant clouds, said, 'Mam? She's in the moon, isn't she?' And then he ran back up the hill, only stopping when Nia couldn't reach him, even with a word.

She didn't shout, 'That can't be true!' for with Emlyn, she felt, anything could be true.

She began to walk down the deserted street, peering in doorways, behind trees, post boxes and a telephone kiosk. The star-spangled shoes were nowhere to be seen.

Ivor Griffiths' Landrover was parked in the road outside Number 6, and Nia hoped his presence would occupy her parents' attention while she slipped unnoticed into the house.

But it was not to be.

'Nia Lloyd! What on earth? Where've you been, I'd like to know?' Her mother was in the hall, her face white and angry, and her pretty smock covered in dust. 'If I didn't know you better I'd have had the police out. Nerys went looking and found my best shoes in the gutter!'

'But you don't wear them now,' Nia said quietly.

Mrs Lloyd stamped her foot. 'That's not the point, is it?'

Mr Lloyd emerged from the kitchen mumbling, 'What's this? What's this? Close the door, it's gone cold!'

He was closely followed by Ivor Griffiths and three boys
with jam on their faces, eager to witness a scolding.

Confined in the dark hall, Fly began to growl.

'Good God, girl! What d'you think you're doing in that
stuff?' Mr Lloyd seized Fly's lead. 'Where've you been,
all got up like a . . . like a prize cake!'

Iolo and the twins began to giggle, but Nia lifting her
head, said, 'I think I look quite nice, really. Anyway
Emlyn Llewelyn's dad thought I did!'

'What? You haven't been up there?'

'It's beautiful!'

All at once her parents, and even Ivor Griffiths, began
to chatter low and nervously. They were upset, Nia could
feel it. They didn't want to alarm her but their restraint
was far more frightening. Her mother gently removed the
red hat and the beads, and started to undo the shell-belt,
all the while murmuring, 'You won't go there again, love,
will you? It's best not to! Promise you won't!'

Nia nodded. She was shivering and wriggling her nose
because she couldn't understand them, but she was careful
not to make a promise. She knew she would go to the
chapel again, whatever they said.

'You do as Mam says!' Mr Griffiths added his advice in
a grave and gravelly voice.

Taking her assent for granted, her father and Mr
Griffiths retreated to the kitchen, herding Fly and the boys
before them.

Nia stepped out of the violet dress and her mother
gathered it up, with the beads and the belt. 'I'm going to
put these away now, my love,' she said, 'and I don't want
you to wear them again for a bit.'

'Even in the house?' Nia asked, dismayed.

'No, your dad doesn't like it!'

'But, Mam . . . '

'I'm putting them away,' Mrs Lloyd said firmly. 'No more dressing-up for a while,' and she whisked her bright bundle up the stairs.

'Where are you taking them, Mam?' Nia cried frantically, leaping after her mother, two steps at a time. 'I may need them.'

'No, you won't!' Her mother was already far above her, on the narrow stairs that led to the third floor and her own bedroom. 'Wash your hands and go and have your tea!'

A door slammed.

Alone on the landing, Nia clenched her fists with frustration and cried, 'Oh! Oh! Oh!'

Alun came out of his room, followed by Gwyn Griffiths. 'Did you get a row?' Alun asked with some sympathy.

'A bit!' said Nia staring at Gwyn Griffiths. She was surprised to see him so soon after the move from Tŷ Llŷr.

'I came with Dad!' Gwyn returned Nia's stare. 'To help unpack and that!'

Nia did not believe him. Upset as she was, she noticed a conspiratorial air about the boys. Gwyn had come to see Alun about something; and it must be very important, and secret.

'Gwyn brought a cake from his mam,' Alun said. 'It's great! Go and have some!'

Nia was not put off the scent. Something unusual had happened; Gwyn looked so tense. 'Come with me!' she said.

Alun was about to refuse, but Gwyn nudged him and said, 'We've had our tea, but we'll eat some more,' and he led the way downstairs

Nerys and Catrin were doing the washing-up when they went into the kitchen. The crockery had been unpacked

37

but not put away and waited in precarious piles around the room.

'You don't deserve cake, Nia Lloyd' said Nerys. 'A lot of bother you've caused today. It isn't as if we didn't have enough to do, without going looking for you.'

'Nia-can't-do-nothing! Nia-in-the . . . ' the twins began.

'Now then! Now then!' Mr Lloyd intervened. 'It's all over. Come for some more is it, boys? Sit down, then. By golly, your wife bakes a grand cake, Ivor!'

'She does indeed!' Mr Griffiths agreed. He wasn't a man given to long speeches but on the subject of his wife's talent he was always more than generous. 'She's a grand cook, Glenys is; she can bake anything, never fails; wins prizes at Pendewi show every year.'

'Every year,' Mr Lloyd repeated, on cue.

'And so would our mam if she wasn't washing all day,' sad loyal Catrin, placing a large slice of sponge cake on Nia's plate. 'Aren't you cold, just in a T-shirt, Nia? Your arms are blue.'

Nia shook her head, her mouth full of cake. She was cold but cake was more important than cardigans.

'What's happened to the weather?' grumbled Mr Lloyd. 'There'll be a frost tonight I shouldn't wonder, and it was so hot today.'

If Nia hadn't been looking to see if Alun's slice of cake was larger than her own, she wouldn't have noticed his expression; as it was she was just in time to see him lift his eyebrows, very slightly, and glance at Gwyn and she suddenly remembered the terrible cold, nearly two years ago, just after Gwyn had come flying down the lane past Tŷ Llŷr, shouting that he was a magician. No one believed him, of course and, for a while even Alun wouldn't speak to him. And then everything went wrong. A great storm had blown up from nowhere. Sheep had died and Alun had got lost on the mountain – it had disappeared in a cloud of snow; no one could get through. It was a phenomenon they said, but they didn't talk about it much. Alun had been found and after that he believed Gwyn. But Nia had always believed, right from the beginning, and when she looked at Gwyn she could feel the excitement in him, half-afraid, half-yearning, and she knew something would happen again, quite soon.

'I saw your cousin today, Gwyn!' she said brightly.

Gwyn frowned at his plate. 'Which cousin?'

'Emlyn Llewelyn,' Nia said.

Gwyn looked at his father, who was staring at him. 'Who says he's my cousin?'

'Mr Llewelyn.'

'What's so special about seeing Emlyn, he lives here, doesn't he?' Alun said accusingly. Nia got the impression that he was trying to defend Gwyn.

'I just thought . . .'

Before she could finish her sentence Mrs Lloyd sang out from the hall, 'Bath, Iolo! Come on!' and bustled in, carrying a bundle of clean clothes.

'Why me first?' Iolo complained, just as he always did.

'You're the youngest! You're the youngest!' the twins chanted, just as they always did.

'Just imagine,' said Catrin. 'You'll be first in the new bath, Iolo!'

That did it.

'Can we get in too?' Changing their tune, the twins rushed out after Iolo and their mother, and the room immediately became a little larger.

'We'd better get going, Gwyn.' Mr Griffiths stood up

39

and tapped his son on the shoulder. 'We haven't fed the animals.'

'I'll get the dog!' said Mr Lloyd.

Nia thought nothing of her father's words until she heard Fly barking, and then she jumped up crying, 'Dog? You're not taking our dog?'

'She's a good dog,' said Mr Griffiths, 'and not happy here. She'll be better at our place.'

'No! No!' Nia ran into the hall. 'You never said, Dad. You never told me.'

'What's got into you, girl?' her father retorted impatiently. Fly was sitting by the door, ready to go, all neat and alert, like someone going to a new school. 'Mr Griffiths agreed to take the dog if I couldn't find another buyer,' Mr Lloyd went on. 'She can't stay here, can she? No sheep, no field; she's as miserable as sin!'

'But I did find a buyer, Dad! I did! I did!'

'And who is that?'

'Emlyn Llewelyn!'

'Don't be daft, Nia! Fly's a sheep-dog, a good one, too; she needs sheep and a farm.'

'But I promised! I promised!' Nia sobbed. 'I can't break my promise, he'll never forgive me.'

Through her tears she saw her father pass Fly's lead to Mr Griffiths; the door opened; the man and the dog stepped out.

Gwyn Griffiths, following his father, looked back, concerned by Nia's outburst. 'You can come and see her,' he said kindly.

'It's not me that wants to, is it?' Nia snapped.

It wasn't the black door that closed then, it was the bright blue door, with golden flowers on it. How could she go back now? They wouldn't want her without the beads and the violet dress. They wouldn't want her without Fly.

'Everything's gone,' she wailed at the door, though her words were meant for her family. 'I've got nothing left! Nothing, nothing, nothing!'

'Course you have, my love,' said her mother from the stairs. 'You've got us, and you've got a nice new home!'

Mam didn't understand!

3
The
Woman
in the
Moon

'It won't do, will it, Nia Lloyd?'

Mr James slammed Nia's exercise book on to her desk. 'Do you call that writing? My eyes ache with the searching, searching for a word I can read!'

Nia regarded her messy indecipherable letters. It was the best she could do.

'You'd better buck up, girl, or it's back to the nursery class for you, isn't it?' Mr James turned away to silence, with a stare, the sniggering that had broken out behind him. He had taken an aspirin to soothe his toothache but any relief he might have expected had been destroyed by the sight of Nia Lloyd's attempt at writing. It was worse than her reading. Was there nothing she could do? Perhaps his long-cherished Project would stir some latent talent in the poor girl.

Mr James, his shoulders significantly braced, his chest puffed out with promise, strolled back to the front of the classroom, where he swung round on his heel and, smiling through swollen gums, delivered his long-awaited announcement.

'And now for the Project!' Mr James exhaled with optimism. 'I want all of you, *all* of you,' he fixed Nia with a cold blue eye, 'to do for me, a piece of work on our glorious little patch of Wales; our town and environment. Write a story!' He flourished with his left hand. 'Draw a picture, make a painting, compose a song!' Here, several flourishes with his right hand sent papers flying from his desk. Undeterred and in full steam now, Mr James pounded to his climax, 'And at the end of term, we'll have an exhibition, a bit of a show, in the library, for everyone to see.'

If she had dared, Nia would have rested her head on her desk in despair. She could already feel the humiliation that was bound to come when her inevitably messy work was exposed to the world. Mr James was watching her while he rattled on about mountains and monuments, about the Celtic magicians, Gwydion, Math and Gilfaethwy and the heroes of Wales. Nia could not attend to his words. She could neither paint nor draw, her writing was a mess, and she had absolutely no musical talent. Why could he not leave her in peace?

The bell went and she left the classroom with Gwyneth Bowen.

'What are you going to do, Nia?' Gwyneth was full of the Project. There were not many things that Gwyneth could not do. She was Nia's friend, and also her tormentor.

'Don't know,' Nia mumbled.

'It's a pity you can't draw,' Gwyneth said, as they strolled on to the playground. 'It's easier than writing. I'm going to write a story and illustrate it.'

'I expect it will be the best,' Nia said humbly.'Your work usually is.'

'Yes,' Gwyneth agreed, 'but this time it's going to be fantastic, even for me.'

43

'Well done,' Nia said prematurely. She had noticed a boy detach himself from a group and look in her direction. Emlyn Llewelyn was coming towards them. She had an overwhelming desire to flee from the conversation that would end either with her lying, or with Emlyn turning his back on her for ever. She wanted, so much, to talk to him, and she wanted, above all, to go back to the chapel.

'Hullo, Nia!' Emlyn's voice was casual but his eyes were anxious. 'Did you talk to your dad?'

'Yes!' That, at least, was true!

'What did he say?'

'He . . . he isn't sure.'

'What are you talking about?' Gwyneth disapproved of Emlyn; she didn't know why, unless it was because her mother did, and he didn't go on school trips or wear the special school T-shirt.

'A dog,' Nia explained. 'Emlyn's going to buy our sheep-dog.'

'You can't keep a sheep-dog,' said Gwyneth scornfully. 'You haven't got sheep.'

'We've a field,' Emlyn said quietly.

'Huh!' Gwyneth sauntered away to join more congenial friends.

'Will you come and see us after school?' Emlyn asked. 'Dad wants to finish your portrait, and can you bring Fly?'

'Mam's taken the clothes. She doesn't want me to wear them again.'

'Doesn't matter. Just bring the dog!' Emlyn ran off and was lost in the crowded playground before Nia could reply.

She spent the rest of her break alone. She sauntered round the playground perimeter, pausing to gaze at games that did not interest her. Her mind was racing. How could

44

she get away to the chapel again? Would Emlyn discover her lie too soon? Would Gwyn Griffiths tell? No, he never spoke to Emlyn. And why was that? Why?

Nia was quite incapable of concentrating on the afternoon activities. Fortunately she was blessed with an hour of singing practice, when she could move her mouth in appropriate directions without making a sound, something that did not require a great deal of effort on her part for she was, by now, quite practised at it.

At home her abstraction went unnoticed. There was still so much to be done. So many pieces to fit into new places. The ancient dark furniture, which had seemed so much a part of Tŷ Llŷr, looked awkward and overpowering here. Cupboards obscured windows, tables protruded through doorways, jam-jars mounted the stairs like sentinels – no walk-in larder here – no room for pickled damsons and plum jam at Number 6.

The old dresser seemed to occupy more than half the kitchen. It regarded the family with sadness and disapproval as they sat, squashed in their chairs, beneath its dark brooding presence. But none of them would have been prepared to do without it, for hadn't it been made by Mam's great-great-grandfather Llŷr, a hundred and fifty years ago?

When Nia had helped with the washing-up she informed her mother she was 'going to see Gwyneth for a bit'.

'Which Gwyneth?' Mrs Lloyd inquired.

'Her mam's Mrs Bowen that sells the wool and buttons and stuff like that,' Nia said happily, for this part was all true. 'She said I could go and visit any time. Gwyneth doesn't get on too well with her brother, see, and it'll be nice for her to have company like me!'

45

'You're not going to the chapel, are you?' Suddenly doubtful, Mrs Lloyd looked at her daughter.

'Why would I? Fly's gone.'

'Go and fetch your anorak then, the evenings are still cool. And don't be long.'

Nia dashed up to her room, grabbed her anorak from its hook, and ran back to the landing. Here, however, she did not descend the stairs, but slipped off her shoes and tiptoed up to the third floor. The door that stood open before her revealed a room bursting with boxes; the new nursery, waiting to be decorated. Nia opened the second door and peeped into her parents' room. It was filled with their enormous bed. How the bed had reached its lofty, inaccessible position she could not imagine, but there it was, huge and magnificent, with its patterned posts and patchwork cover, taking up all but a few centimetres between the wardrobe and the wall. If she stood on the bed she would be able to reach the tiny scrap of violet that her mother had failed to conceal behind a row of jars on top of the wardrobe.

Nia withdrew her head and listened to the house: Catrin practising scales in the front room; the boys making explosive noises in the throes of a war game; her parents watching television in the kitchen. Nerys had gone to the library, open late on Mondays. There was no one to spy on Nia.

She leapt upon the big bed and stretched upwards. A jar wobbled dangerously and then was still. Nia extended two fingers between the jars; she could feel a piece of material. She gave a little tug; the jars rattled. She tugged again, very gently, and the violet dress slithered past the jars and dropped on to her head.

Nia jumped off the bed and thrust the dress inside her

47

anorak which she zipped up to her neck. Then she half-ran, half-slithered down the steep and shiny wooden staircase. Pausing on the landing to step into her shoes, she confidently tip-tapped down the second flight of stairs.

She was about to open the front door when her father came out of the kitchen. 'You still here, girl?' he asked, glancing out of the kitchen at her bulging anorak.

'Couldn't find my anorak.' Nia answered.

'Don't go into Llewelyn's chapel, girl,' Mr Lloyd said earnestly. 'No good will come of it.'

'But why, Dad? What's the matter with it?' Nia had to ask.

'Something happened there, didn't it?'

Before Nia could question him further, Mr Lloyd had escaped into his shop.

She opened the front door and stepped out into the quiet street. Bowen's Wool Shop was only three doors away, next to the house where tiny Miss Olwen Oliver turned truants into choirboys, and skinny girls into stars of the opera. Nia decided she would visit Gwyneth, just for a moment, so that if she was questioned later, she could truthfully answer that she had seen her friend.

Gwyneth was not at home and there was no answer to Nia's insistent knocking. She would have to risk a lie.

There was a light in the chapel, but Nia's first timid knock went unheard and, reluctant to intrude, she climbed on to the lowest rung of the pink and gold railings and peeped into the window. Emlyn was kneeling on the floor beside an oil-lamp; he was absorbed in one of his animals, in an attitude of such repose he might have been a statue himself. The only movement came from a small knife in his hand, that flashed now and then, in the lamplight. Mr Llewelyn was nowhere to be seen.

48

Nia stepped down from the railings, climbed the steps that led to the blue door, and knocked again. The door was opened, a few seconds later, by Emlyn. He seemed pleased to see her. 'What did your dad say about the dog?' he asked.

'He's thinking about it.'

'Good.' Emlyn held the door wider to let her pass.

Nia looked uncertainly at the figure, hunched by a window before his easel.

'Don't worry about him,' Emlyn drew her in and closed the door. 'He's in a bad mood. Work's not going well.' He spoke as though his father were not aware of them.

Nia decided to adopt Emlyn's attitude. 'What's he painting?'

'I don't know – patterns. Someone commissioned it, someone from London. So we'll have a feast when it's finished. They're paying a thousand pounds. I'll get new trainers.'

Nia regarded the worn straps of leather stretched across Emlyn's bare toes. She had thought that he wore sandals from choice. 'Will you have roast beef for your feast?' she asked. 'There's beef hanging in our place, and pigs, all slit open with the blood dripping out.'

A look of horror passed over Emlyn's face. Nia realized how grim her words must have sounded. She hadn't meant to shock; she just wanted to voice her disapproval of Mr Lloyd's new trade.

'We don't eat meat!' Emlyn said.

'I don't like it either,' Nia said quickly. 'It smells, doesn't it?' she added for good measure. 'But I have to eat it, Dad being a butcher an' that.'

Emlyn looked relieved. Nia could not be held responsible for the food that was forced upon her.

'Pwy sydd yna?' The Welsh words came low and weary through the darkening chapel. Nia had almost forgotten Mr Llewelyn.

'It's Nia!' Emlyn said. 'The girl with the dog.' He crouched back on to the floor and picked up his knife.

'Ble mae'r ci? Where is the dog?'

'I – I couldn't bring her today,' Nia grasped for words that would not utterly condemn her when her treachery was discovered.

'And where are the pink shoes that you promised with stardust on them?' Mr Llewelyn's dark features were not fierce. He seemed more like a tired but kindly beast, ambling towards her through his jungle of exotic animals.

'Mam hid them,' Nia said, 'and the hat and the beads. I've brought the dress though.' She unzipped her anorak and proudly displayed her loot.

'It's too dark now,' Emlyn's father sighed and looked over her head. 'What a sky. Like slate it is'

They don't want me, Nia thought; don't need me without the dog. The dress is not enough.

'Have some soup! It's ready!' Emlyn, absorbed in his carving, seemed to make the invitation as a matter of course, rather than a genuine desire for her company.

Undeterred by his indifference, Nia said, 'Yes, please!' and just in case she seemed too eager, 'I didn't have much tea; it was ham, see!'

Mr Llewelyn went to the stove and poured three bowls of soup. It was hot and thick, and rather too green for Nia's liking, but she decided she could get used to it.

They sat cross-legged on the floor to drink their soup, even Mr Llewelyn, and it didn't matter that no one spoke. They didn't grasp for words, search for a subject with which to entertain each other; and Nia felt so comfortable in the silence, she began to wonder at her contentment, and in wondering broke the spell and remembered the Project. She began to cough and couldn't stop until Mr Llewelyn patted her on the back. Even then she still gulped for air, red in the face and breathless.

'Hold on, girl. I'll get you some water!' Emlyn's father went to the sink.

'It isn't just the soup, is it?' Emlyn looked hard at her. 'Something came into your mind to spoil the taste. It does that with me, sometimes. What was the thing that made you cough?'

Nia sipped the water that was handed to her, and while Mr Llewelyn knelt to give them slivers of coarse brown bread, she said, 'It's the Project, Mr James's Project!' And, with a sigh, she unburdened herself and told her hosts of all her problems with Mr James and his desire to exhibit the classroom's work on their environment.

'He's a real pain, that Mr James,' Emlyn remarked sympathetically. 'He's always on about exhibitions; can't leave you alone. I'm glad I'm in Miss Powell's class now.'

'I'm hopeless,' said Nia wistfully. 'They'll all laugh whatever I do. Nia-can't-do-nothing, that's what my brothers call me.'

Mr Llewelyn threw back his head and roared with laughter.

'It's not funny,' Nia said, offended.

'It is, you know.' Mr Llewelyn was still chuckling, but seeing the childrens' reproachful glances added, 'Not you, though, Nia. It doesn't make sense, you see, Nia-can't-do-nothing. If Nia *can't* do nothing, then Nia *can* do something, see!'

Nia thought she saw, but knowing that her brothers used bad grammar didn't solve her problem.

And then Emlyn repeated, 'Nia-*can*-do-something; everyone can do something!'

'Not me!' Nia said gloomily.

'Don't be so pessimistic. You grow flowers, you said. You can see colours, feel them. I know you can.'

'What d'you do at home, girl?' asked Mr Llewelyn, inspired by his son's enthusiasm. 'Can you knit, make things? What d'you do to help your mam?'

'I darn the socks,' Nia said doubtfully. 'I'm quite good at that, actually!'

'There you are then,' said Mr Llewelyn. 'Sew a picture, make fields and mountains from cloth and cotton.'

'Something silver for the river, tinsel maybe, and wool for the clouds,' Emlyn went on eagerly.

'And flowers,' said Nia. 'Mam's got dusters, bright yellow, and old sheets cut up for rags, but still white as anything. Perhaps I can do it.'

'Of course you can, girl. You've got imagination.' Mr Llewelyn leapt to his feet, and gathered up their empty soup bowls. 'I'll find you a piece of canvas, big enough for a masterpiece, and you can sew your shapes to it.'

He dropped the bowls into the sink and began to search among the empty frames and unfinished paintings that leant against the wall, six or seven deep. Suddenly, in the shifting and searching, one of Emlyn's paintings appeared. Nia found herself looking at a woman hanging in the moon; not hanging, perhaps, but stretching up against the lower half of a crescent, as one might do when clinging to a fairground creature on a roundabout. Her hair was black and her long pale dress floated out and round the moon like a cloud. Nia knew who it was, but all the same she asked, 'Who is that?'

And Emlyn answered, as she knew he would, 'It's my

mam!'

'Did you do it?'

'Yes, I did; after she went, two years ago.'

Nia wanted to ask about the moon and why the woman was hanging there, but the painting vanished under another and Mr Llewelyn stepped towards them with a long roll of something. He held one end and unfurled two metres of dusty canvas, filling the air with tiny lamplit particles that glowed and drifted round their heads.

'Here it is then; the background for your picture, Nia.' Mr Llewelyn laid the canvas beside her and stepped away.

'But it's so big!' Nia exclaimed.

'A masterpiece must be large,' he replied. 'I have a feeling about this canvas,' Emlyn's father went on. 'I think you will find yourself here. But keep it out of sight until it is complete. It must be yours, all yours. If you need help, ask us; no one else. And one day, we will see here the true and special Nia!'

'Thank you!' Nia stood up and stared uncertainly at the huge rectangle at her feet.

'Well, take it, girl!' commanded Idris Llewelyn. 'Roll it up and conceal it somewhere about you.'

'But the dress; I can't hide them both in my anorak.'

'Leave the dress here,' Emlyn suggested, 'and fetch it when you bring the dog. Will it be soon?'

'I expect so.' Nia wished he hadn't mentioned Fly. She was taking their gift under false pretences. She knelt and folded the canvas, tucking it guiltily into her anorak, like a thief who knows he is observed but has gone too far to save himself.

'You look so glum, girl,' Mr Llewelyn remarked. 'Cheer up! This is the beginning. Can you use an iron?'

Nia nodded and got to her feet.

'Iron the creases out of your canvas when no one is about, and then hide it; right?'

'I'll do that,' said Nia. 'I'd better go now, and thank you for the soup and . . . and everything.'

'Damn the sky!' Mr Llewelyn was, once again, preoccupied with his own work. 'The light is going and I should have had another two hours.'

Emlyn followed Nia out of the chapel and began to accompany her down the hill.

'I'll be all right,' Nia said.

'I'll come anyway,' he replied and fell into step beside her.

'What's your mam's name?' Nia asked, hoping to forestall any inquiries about Fly.

'Elinor,' he said.

'That's a beautiful name. Why do you think she's in the moon?'

'She told me!'

And then, without any prompting, Emlyn began to tell Nia of the night his mother left; of the howling wind that tore slates from the chapel roof and sent them banging against the windows; the baby crying and his father roaring in the dark, because there were no lights. 'But I could see them both,' Emlyn said softly, 'the moon was so bright, and my mam was walking up and down and round the wooden animals, pushing at them, like she hated them. I fell asleep while they were still rowing and then, much later, she woke me. She said she was taking the baby and leaving my dad; she wanted me to go with her, but I said no. I couldn't leave my dad, could I? And then she said something. ". . . Yr Hanner Lleuad", the half moon, that's all I heard because of the wind; so I painted her in the moon, in a crescent moon, because that's what she said.

But I never told my dad why and he never asked.'

They were no longer walking, but now and again placing one foot in front of the other, until, at last, they stopped moving altogether and Nia said, 'She just went, like that, in the middle of the night?'

'She just went,' he replied.

Nia felt he had left something out, perhaps the most important thing of all; but she had no right to ask any more questions, for she had broken her promise and, even now, when she knew he had probably confided more to her than to anyone, she could not bring herself to tell him the truth about Fly.

The sky was, indeed, like slate; heavy and damp, it pressed all around them, holding the shape of fields and mountains fixed and dark in the distance. Emlyn looked away to a lamplit window at the top of the hill. 'I stood on my bed after she'd gone,' he said, 'and I looked out of the window. There was a Landrover in the road, and a man beside it.'

Nia gasped. 'D'you know who it was?' she asked.

'Yes,' said Emlyn. 'I knew him all right. It was Mr Griffiths, Gwyn's dad. He took my mother away.'

Nia looked hard into his eyes, willing him to smile and tell her that it was not so, not Gwyn's father, but the gaze he steadfastly returned was so grave and so sad that she had to believe him. And then, all at once, he burst out, 'They blame him; blame my dad for driving my mam away. But it's all a lie. She went, didn't she? She didn't have to go. My dad gave her a home, with pictures on the wall and a butterfly ceiling for her baby. She didn't have to go. And they blame me too, for staying. "A boy should go with his mother," they said, but I couldn't, could I? Couldn't leave my dad?'

Emlyn who had seemed so confident, was shaking his head from side to side like a sleepless child, and Nia knew that her answer really mattered. Could she manage, just for once to get it right? 'No,' she said calmly, 'you couldn't leave your dad; he'd be alone.'

Emlyn smiled, almost apologetically, and Nia knew that she had chosen her words wisely.

'I'll come all the way with you tonight,' Emlyn said. 'There are spooks in the air.'

They laughed and then they ran; ran all the way to Number 6, where Emlyn held his nose and made hideous faces at the butcher's dark and empty window, and Nia giggled as she rang the bell. Someone had latched the door. Nerys opened it with a book in one hand. 'I saw your friend Gwyneth in the library,' she said.

'Yes, her dad let me in and I waited!' Nia decided that Gwyneth's father was not likely to frequent libraries. 'We had a great time. Gwyneth's got a new doll's house.'

'She's spoiled,' said Nerys. Her spectacles had slipped to the end of her nose and she didn't see Emlyn, dancing in the street, thumbs in his ears and feet turned out like Charlie Chaplin. 'What're you grinning at, idiot?'

'Nothing,' Nia replied. She followed her sister into the house and turned to give Emlyn a secret signal of farewell.

Emlyn had stopped dancing. He was staring into the hall, listening to the cheerful sounds beyond: the singing, shouting and laughter. He reminded Nia of a hungry, golden-eyed animal, searching for warmth.

She hated closing the door.

4
A
Fight

It was a cold night. The grey clouds drifted south and the moon sailed out, bright and startling from behind the mountains. Falling through frosted glass, it filled the yellow bathroom with soft light and Nia, sleepless with impatience, knew that she had found a safe and secret place to do her work.

Iolo was not easily disturbed from sleep; his face was pressed against his blue monster and his breathing was calm and even as his sister crawled beneath her bed to retrieve the canvas from its hiding place. Nevertheless she tiptoed through the door and dared not shut it tight behind her.

Beside the bath, in the brightest patch of moonlight, Nia spread her canvas and gazed at it. She had managed to iron it in the tiny upstairs room, on the board her mother had left unattended while she ran Iolo's bath. Nia stroked the rough surface and screwed up her eyes, silently demanding the canvas to show her where and how to begin. A huge rectangle of dull brown stared back at her, giving no advice, no encouragement.

Once again, the hateful and familiar feeling of hopelessness began to overwhelm Nia. She sank back on her heels, numb with disappointment. She was not what they thought after all. She could not see shapes and colours where they did not exist. She was not gifted with imagination. The Llewelyns had burdened her with a talent she did not possess. They expected too much.

Motionless, she crouched on the cold floor until the church clock struck twice. The lonely, hollow sound made her shiver. It was time to put away the masterpiece that would never be.

A wisp of cloud passed across the moon; the long dress of a lady in the sky. A shadow covered the canvas like a ghost and, when it had gone, a faint shape appeared beside Nia's cold hand where it touched the frayed edge. The pale form gathered strength and colour, it became a roof, dark grey, with a chimney in the centre. Another roof emerged beside the first, dark red this one, with a curl of smoke drifting from the chimney-pot. The lower edge of the canvas began to fill with imaginary shapes and colours. Nia was so excited she ran to the bedroom, crashing the door back against Iolo's toy box. The rhythm of her brother's quiet breathing changed, but he did not wake.

Nia opened a cupboard and took out her sewing basket. She found a large needle, scissors, and a ball of soft grey wool. Terrified that the picture in her mind would evaporate before she could commit it to canvas, she rushed back to the bathroom, slipped on the shiny floor, and crashed into a stool, sending it spinning into the bath. In the silent house, the noise seemed deafening. For a whole minute Nia waited, frozen, against the wall. When she had assured herself that she had not woken her family she knelt beside her canvas and began to thread the needle. This done, she made three tiny stitches in the material. She paused to consider, then made a long stitch, then a curve.

Nia teased the wool with the sharp end of her needle and pale grey, drifting smoke appeared.

'Oh!' she sighed, surprised and delighted by her achievement.

'Nia?'

Someone had been disturbed after all. Catrin stood in the open doorway.

'Can't you sleep?'

It was too late to hide the canvas. 'Something woke me!' Nia said.

'What's that on the floor?'

'Nothing – just a piece of stuff I found; I'm . . . I'm sewing on it. Please don't tell.'

'I won't tell, but you'd better go to bed now or you'll never wake up in the morning.' Kind Catrin never scolded.

Nia smiled and rolled up her work. She had begun. Nothing mattered now. The smoke was there and it would remain. Tomorrow there would be a chimney and a roof and perhaps pink blossom on a tree. 'I'll sleep now,' she said happily.

Catrin followed Nia to her room and smoothed the pillow. 'You're a funny one,' she said as Nia climbed into bed.

'I'm glad it wasn't Nerys who found me,' Nia whispered.

'I bet you are!' Catrin began to tidy the rumpled sheets. Before she had finished, Nia was asleep.

There began a week of feverish activity for Nia. Scraps of cotton, corduroy and velvet were begged from her mother and retrieved from rag-bags, boxes and bottom drawers. Christmas paper, tinsel and ribbons were carefully acquired from friends and neighbours. Gwyneth Bowen came up trumps and donated a whole box of shop-soiled wool and her mother's tired satin petticoat. She didn't even ask what they were for.

All these precious bits Nia hoarded, mouse-like, in plastic bags beneath her bed. And no one guessed, no one asked, no one wanted to know what she was up to!

Luckily Mrs Lloyd had never been a great one for 'doing out' bedrooms, and the hoard grew undisturbed, until there was scarcely enough room for the canvas which Nia rolled with great care every night, after she had smoothed bits of material, snipped loose threads and ensured that glue was dry.

She forgot about Fly and her broken promise. Her mind was filled with the colour and complexion of the world about her; the intensity of shadows, shades of the sky, the brilliance of flowers and curving shapes of trees. She was completely enthralled by her new occupation, though she managed to chat to Gwyneth and play hopscotch while counting windows.

And then, one day, when the canvas lay safe and secret under her bed, already half-filled with patches, Nia was forced to remember Fly. She was standing in the middle of the playground, gazing up, through half-closed eyes, at a giant yew in the churchyard beyond the school wall.

She was hardly aware of the activity about her, until someone began to approach and Emlyn Llewelyn broke through a hazy foreground.

I can ask him about the yew, she thought; he'll know if it's green or black. But when she had made sense of his expression she realized that she could ask him nothing. He had discovered her treachery.

When he knew he had Nia's attention, Emlyn stood

very still; his golden eyes were dangerous and his words quiet and cold.

'Why didn't you tell me about the dog?'

'I didn't know . . . I wasn't sure, I . . . I couldn't . . .'

'You promised!'

Nia shook her head hopelessly. 'My dad did it. I told him about . . . about you, wanting the dog an' all, but it was too late!'

'You let *them* have it, and you never told me!' Emlyn's voice began to rise.

A crowd of children, sensing conflict, gathered closer.

'Why Gwyn Griffiths? Why not me? You knew I wanted the dog. You knew how much I wanted her.'

Nia looked away from him. She had been prepared for anger; it was his humiliation that she could not endure.

'Look at me,' Emlyn cried, and, turning, Nia saw his hand go to his pocket and pull out a strip of leather. 'I even bought a lead. Stupid, wasn't it? A lead and no dog. I don't need it now, do I?'

Emlyn raised his arm. For a moment the strip of leather hung innocently from his hand and then, suddenly, it came snaking towards Nia as she stood awaiting her punishment.

But someone stepped in front of her and Nia heard gasps of horror and delight as the hard leather struck Gwyn Griffiths in the face. An angry red mark appeared on his cheek and he walked towards Emlyn, holding the lead tight in his hand.

Emlyn stood his ground for a moment, angry and unrepentant, then he turned and ran.

Gwyn pursued him slowly at first, but as Emlyn approached the low playground wall, Gwyn gathered speed. Emlyn flung himself at the wall and tumbled over

61

into the narrow lane between the churchyard and the playground. Gwyn followed only seconds after, and Nia found that she was running too, knowing that whatever was going to happen would be her fault.

'Nia Lloyd, where are you going?' called Miss Powell, on duty by the climbing frame and more concerned with death-defying five-year-olds than Nia Lloyd's flight. She hadn't even noticed the boys.

'You'll catch it when you get back!' someone called as Nia fell, breathless, into the stony lane.

She caught sight of Gwyn turning on to the path that led to the churchyard and stumbled after him. Her mind was racing her feet and they would not obey her. She could not keep her balance; twice she tripped and crashed on to the stones. 'You'll catch it!' warned the sing-song voices, Gwyneth Bowen's louder than the rest.

Nia reached a swinging wrought-iron gate. The voices faded. She hesitated. Beyond lay the graveyard; not her favourite place. It was dark with ancient trees; a place where long ago, before any church was built, men had prayed to gods other than the one she knew.

She braced herself and passed through the gate. A shroud of trees enveloped her as she walked down the avenue, soft with moss and weeds. She watched and listened for signs of battle, but there were none. Perhaps the two boys had parted without a fight, yet she could not believe it.

There were five yews in the churchyard, all of them a thousand years old, so it was said, and Nia could believe it. Their hollow trunks were scarred and dusty, their branches of dark needles bent and cracked. Mysterious trees, sacred and poisonous.

She left the path and allowed herself to be drawn further

out into the maze of older graves; into a place inhabited by phantoms whose names could not be read, and where the yews trailed damp fingers over decaying stones. The feeling of unseen and mysterious power never left her, and she wondered why Emlyn had chosen such a retreat.

On a patch of dead ground, beneath the furthest, darkest tree, Nia saw the boys. Or rather she saw one form, circling slowly. They were closed in combat, their tangled arms embracing, their legs hardly moving. The black head tight against the brown and their bodies pushing, unremittingly, one against the other. And then one boy broke free, Emlyn, and he began to beat his adversary with desperate and deadly fists.

Gwyn reeled back, defending himself with upraised arms. Emlyn was the taller and more powerful boy, but

63

Nia sensed a strength about Gwyn that could withstand
and even overcome the other. And she remembered that
strange time two years ago, when Gwyn had inflicted a
terrible injury on fat Dewi Davis, no one knew how. They
said a stone had been thrown and broken Dewi's nose, but
Nia had seen no stone; she believed Gwyn had a power
that could not be named; once, he had called himself a
magician.

The magician was kneeling now, shielding his head with
his hands. Emlyn seized him by the shoulders and would
have thrown him over, but something happened. The
kneeling boy seemed to lose his shape, or change it.

Emlyn stepped back, his eyes fixed on Gwyn, utterly
astonished; and he kept on stepping back until he was
almost lost in the gloom beneath the tree. And when he

stopped moving the two boys were frozen in a great bowl of nothingness where no birds sang, no leaves fell, and even dust was motionless. And Nia was standing on the very edge, breathing, but only just. She wanted to scream, but something was strangling sound.

Then Gwyn stood up, his arms raised, fingers stretched wide, like a cat spreading its claws. A boy who was not a boy, but a part of the magic in the sacred yews and of the ageless shadows beneath them. All the dark power that still dwelt in the graveyard seemed to have gathered into his hands.

And then he let it go. His arms dropped to his sides, and something fell away from him, an unseen mantle that he had borrowed from the air in a moment of need.

Emlyn, released, sprang forward and felled his enemy with one blow.

He ran past Nia, scarcely seeing her. The victor. But his face showed repentance and when he reached the path, she thought she heard a sob.

Gwyn got to his feet, rubbing his head. An ordinary boy who had been hurt, but Nia still felt in awe of him. She walked towards him, meaning to thank him for defending her, but instead she asked, 'Why did you let him beat you?'

'He's stronger,' Gwyn said.

'No he isn't! You can do things to the air. It's frightening!'

Gwyn gave her a sly look, the sort of look he usually reserved for Alun. She felt privileged.

'Emlyn had to win,' was all he said.

Nia understood. 'He is your cousin, isn't he?' She looked sideways at him.

Gwyn sighed. 'Yes, he's my cousin. But he hates me,

and it isn't just the dog.' He closed his eyes and rubbed his forehead. 'There's something wrong between our families.'

'Your father stole his mother!' Nia said quietly

'That's not true!' he sounded angry, but astonished at the solution to an old and painful puzzle. 'It can't be true . . . ' his voice trailed off and then he added softly, 'I didn't know. Why didn't he tell me?' and then again, 'It's not true!'

Nia was glad that he hadn't known; hadn't been part of the plot. 'It is true,' she said. 'The way Emlyn told it to me . . . he couldn't have made it up!'

They began to walk towards the church, their feet making no sound on the damp yew needles.

'My dad's secretive,' Gwyn murmured, 'he's deep, but he always has a reason. Where did he take Emlyn's mam then?'

'Emlyn says she's in the moon.'

Gwyn didn't laugh, he just said, 'She was my Auntie Elinor. She was beautiful and very special to Bethan.'

'Your sister?'

'Yes; she went . . .'

Nia thought he was going to tell her where, but he continued, ' . . . nearly five years ago. Disappeared. And then my Auntie Elinor,' Gwyn was almost speaking to himself. 'They'd just come back from somewhere, the Llewelyns; France, I think it was. Emlyn was born out there, I didn't know him. Bethan really took to Elinor, they used to plant seeds together, and pick wild flowers and press them in a book. Then, in November, Bethan went, just after Halloween. We didn't see much of the Llewelyns after that. Dad was, well, sick or something. And soon after, Auntie Elinor went away and Dad told me my Uncle Idris was wicked and I was never to speak to him or Emlyn again, they weren't relations any more.'

'Emlyn isn't wicked!' Nia said.

Gwyn shrugged. 'I've gone to the same school,' he said, 'and I've sat in the same room, and since then I've never spoken to him till today.'

'Did you speak today?'

Gwyn frowned. 'No,' he said, surprised by his answer. 'But we fought and that's like speaking, in a way.'

'It was my fault, all of it!' Nia said.

'No it wasn't. I had to defend you, and myself. I had to pay him back for being mad, he expected it.'

They were on the path now, and leaving the trees. The playground was near but unusually quiet. They had almost reached the churchyard gate when Nia found the courage to ask, 'Gwyn, you told us once that you were a magician. Are you one?'

He sighed, thrust his hands deep into his pockets and looked up at the sky. 'Yes,' he said, 'but don't talk about it. It's not always an advantage, being a magician! I have to hide it. It's getting stronger in me, and sometimes I'm afraid I'll get it wrong; do something, in a moment, without thinking, and then . . . !'

Fearing he had said too much, Gwyn waited for a scornful response. None came. Remembering what had happened beneath the yew, Nia was overawed, and did not know what to say. But instinct told her that Gwyn's power would never hurt Emlyn again.

Beside the gate they saw the dog's lead, where Gwyn had dropped it. He picked it up. 'What shall I do with this?' he muttered.

'Keep it,' Nia said. 'Perhaps you can give it back one day.'

Gwyn put the lead in his pocket. 'Fly might have pups,' he said thoughtfully.

They emerged into sunlight and Nia saw clearly the red stripe across Gwyn's cheek where the leather had lashed it.

'Does your face hurt?' she asked.

'Not much!'

'What are you going to say about the mark?'

'I'll say I had a fight with Nia Lloyd and she beat me!' He laughed and then he ran down the lane away from her.

They soon discovered why the playground was so quiet. In spite of Miss Powell's vigilance, the climbing frame had claimed a victim: one of the Lloyd twins, Gareth, lay moaning on the ground.

5
The
Curtain

Iolo rushed to Nia, when he saw her. 'Where've you been? I wanted you. Gareth's hurt!' he cried.

Before Nia could reply, Siôn was pulling at her skirt and yelling, 'Where've you been? Gareth's had an accident!'

'I can see that,' Nia said sharply. 'I wasn't far away – I'm here now. What happened?'

'He was balancing,' Siôn said proudly. 'It was great. Right on top he was! Miss Powell yelled at him to come down. He'd have been all right if she hadn't yelled.'

Miss Powell was in a bit of a state. She seemed unable to decide whether to scold, comfort or assist the stricken boy. Then Mr James arrived and took control of the situation. He gently felt all Gareth's limbs, picked him up and carried him into the school.

A crowd of children respectfully made way for the patient's relatives. Alun, Nia, Siôn and Iolo, wearing suitably funereal expressions, followed Mr James and their brother. Nia wished that Nerys and Catrin were with them, and not half a mile away at the High School.

Doctor Vaughan arrived and only minutes later, Mrs Lloyd. Gareth was whisked off to hospital, accompanied by his mother. The other Lloyds returned to their separate

69

classrooms, amid sympathetic murmurs from their friends.

'Is it fatal?' Gwyneth inquired in a solemn whisper.

Nia did not deign to reply.

The anxiety that she betrayed when she returned home was misinterpreted by her mother.

Mrs Lloyd had left the hospital, reassured that broken limbs were all the rage for eight-year-old boys.

'Don't fret, cariad. It's only a broken leg. It'll soon mend,' she said when Nia, tears springing to her eyes, had misplaced a glass and let it smash on to the tiled kitchen floor.

Nia felt guilty. Her thoughts were not with Gareth. Emlyn hadn't returned to school that afternoon. Where had he gone and why? He had won a fight, but she could not forget the desolate look on his face when he had passed her, and she could not forget the way Gwyn Griffiths had frozen life in the dim space under the yews, or the red mark on his cheek that should have been on hers.

When she took her canvas to the bathroom that night, there was no moon. The street lamp was bright enough but her picture looked somehow dead in artificial light. She found green corduroy for the yew trees, but couldn't remember their shape, and there was not enough of Alun's old grey socks to make a church.

'I can't do it! I can't do it!' She muttered angrily at the canvas. Nia-can't-do-nothing, who had been absent for a week, was peering over her shoulder, clutching at her hands. She needed to see Emlyn and his father, to ask for their advice and encouragement. Would they ever speak to her again?

When she replaced the canvas under her bed she had not added one stitch to it. Nor did she add any the following night. Emlyn had not been in school.

On the third evening after Gareth's accident, Nia slipped into the boys' bedroom when it was empty, and took a new grey sock from Gareth's drawer.

'He'll only need one now,' she told herself.

That night she tried to cut it into the shape of a church. The frayed pieces stretched and fell apart. Nia sat in the bathroom, glaring at her unfinished collage, remembering that Gareth had not lost a leg but merely broken one. She snipped the grey sock into tiny shreds and flushed them down the lavatory.

'There's something in the toilet,' Nerys complained next morning at breakfast. 'It's grey and it won't flush away.'

'Worms!' said Siôn with relish.

'You're a worm, worm!' Nerys retorted.

'It's a rag – just a rag,' Nia said quickly. 'All cut up.'

'Oh, Nia!' Mrs Lloyd, distracted from scraping burnt toast into the pedal bin, let her foot slip and sooty crumbs flew everywhere. 'Now look what you've made me do. I've told you not to throw things down the toilet.'

Nia wondered if there'd be a hole in the toast after her mother's attack. 'I thought it would go down if I cut it up,' she said meekly.

'Now then, girl. You know better than that. We don't want trouble with the drains again,' said Mr Lloyd, scrubbing his butcher's fingers extra hygienically in the sink.

Emlyn was in school for the first time since the fight. He wouldn't even look in Nia's direction.

She decided to postpone making the church and concentrate on trees, but she didn't know how to make blossom. And then she remembered something.

71

Catrin had a music lesson after school that evening, with Miss Olwen Oliver, always called Olwen to distinguish her from her sister Enid Oliver who ran the bakery and took boarders.

'Can I come with you to Miss Olwen Oliver?' Nia asked her sister.

'Whatever for?'

'I like listening to you play.'

Nia had tried music lessons but had proved unmusical, as Miss Oliver put it.

'What a good idea!' Mrs Lloyd said brightly. Perhaps they had started Nia on a musical career too early. Perhaps, after all, she had talent. 'I'm sure Miss Olwen Oliver wouldn't mind. Nia could sit quietly at the back of the room: it's such a big room, you wouldn't even notice her.'

'Well . . . ' Catrin's blue eyes widened uncertainly.

'Please?' Nia begged.

Gentle Catrin was persuaded.

Ten minutes later Nia found herself sitting exactly where she wanted: at the end of Miss Oliver's long chair-lined music room. The chairs were all of a different size and age, acquired on separate occasions as Miss Oliver's fame and fortune progressed; very few were comfortable. The faded, floral wallpaper was bare except for black-framed certificates and photographs of successful music students at local Eisteddfodau. Apart from the two black pianos and a smell of fish, that was it.

The fish smell was a mystery. Miss Oliver was not even a Roman Catholic and, as far as anyone knew, did hardly enough shopping to keep a bird alive. She was a tiny woman, her face a triangle of carved ivory, with pointed nose and chin, and deep-set black eyes. Her hair, plaited and coiled neatly into the nape of her neck, had been white for so long even *she* could barely remember what colour it had been. All these features paled into insignificance behind Miss Olwen Oliver's truly magnificent eyebrows; long, black and shaggy, they dominated her every expression, controlled every situation, disciplined every six-foot chorister. No one crossed swords with Miss Oliver's eyebrows, if they could help it.

Nia had no intention of taking up piano lessons again; the experience had been far too painful.

Miss Oliver had welcomed her in with a rather predatory gleam, and allowed her to choose a chair. 'Not too close to the piano, now, or it'll be a distraction for Catrin, who is to take an examination soon, isn't she?'

So Nia chose a chair beside the window, as far from the piano as possible. There was a lace curtain in the window, real lace, a beautiful creamy white, like plum blossom. The scalloped hem of the curtain hung a good ten centimetres below the window!

Nia took a pair of tiny sewing scissors out of her skirt pocket. Catrin and her teacher were concentrating on Mozart. It was a very beautiful sonata; it reminded Nia of the music Catrin had played at Tŷ Llŷr. Nia had made her dolls dance under the window where the plum trees made green patches on the thick white wall.

Snip! Snip! Snip! She had severed half the hem of the lace curtain. It was all she needed but the other half looked odd now. She cut to the end of the hem, taking her time and carefully following the curves in the lace. How beautifully the patterns parted, how prettily the scalloped hem brushed the window-sill. She'd done Miss Oliver a favour. Nia slipped the strip of deliciously soft lace into her pocket.

Catrin's music lessons always ended with a small display by Miss Oliver, just to show that, whatever level of excellence her pupils had attained, there was still a long way to go before perfection was achieved.

Almost on cue, Catrin's friend, Mary McGoohan rang the bell on the last note of Miss Oliver's final flourish.

'Shall I open the door for you?' Nia offered.

'There's a kind girl,' tiny Miss Oliver turned and gave a neat smile. 'Perhaps you'd like to have lessons again, Nia?'

'Perhaps.' Nia didn't linger. She was out of the music room and opening the front door before Miss Oliver had closed her trim lips.

'I thought you'd given up the piano, Nia?' said Mary McGoohan.

'I have!' Nia leapt past her and would have run to Number 6 but, remembering to appear calm, waited for Catrin and walked sedately beside her.

Catrin always sang after her music lesson; her voice was very sweet and soothing. There was no one Nia would rather be with. Catrin was restful and undemanding. One day she would be a star, Nia was sure of that; she was tall and golden, like the girl in a picture on the library wall, painted by a fifteenth-century Italian. Catrin was understanding, she never asked questions. Today, however, she did.

'Are you sleeping better now, Nia?'

'Oh yes!' They had reached Number 6. 'That is, more or less,' Nia said cautiously. She opened the black and private door, rushed across the hall and up the stairs to her room.

Iolo's cars were coming for her in single file across the floor, Iolo behind them, making appropriate revving noises. 'Where've you been?' he muttered through the revs.

'Music lesson!' Nia replied. She had expected him to be watching television. Now she couldn't hide the lace in her scrap bags. She stood as close as she could to the chest of drawers, opened the top drawer a fraction and took the lace from her pocket.

'What're you doing?'

'Getting a hanky,' Nia said irritably. She had never known Iolo to be so interested in her movements.

From the bottom of the stairs, Nerys called, 'Tea!' and Iolo, always eager to have first choice of whatever was on the table, leapt up and ran out of the room.

Nia tucked the stolen lace under a pile of white socks and followed him.

It was cold roast beef for tea: Sunday left-overs. Mrs Lloyd put a slice on Nia's plate. The meat stared up at Nia; it was pink in the middle and Nia found herself saying, 'No thanks!'

'What?' her mother didn't seem to understand.

'I don't want any meat, thank you,' Nia said.

'Are you ill, cariad?' Mrs Lloyd's children had never turned down cold roast beef before.

'No, I'm not ill, I'm a vegetarian!' Nia pushed her plate away.

'What?' Her mother stared at her stupidly, her mouth hanging open like a fish.

'I'm a vegetarian,' Nia repeated. '*I don't like meat!*'

The silence that followed reminded her of the time

76

Uncle Maldwyn and Auntie Ann had died, he under his tractor and she an hour later of heart failure. They were nearly eighty but it had still been a shock. Being a vegetarian was surely not so shocking?

The boys began to giggle; Catrin looked embarrassed; Nerys had a sort of 'I told you so' expression on her face. And then the atmosphere dissolved abruptly as a menacing rumble crescendoed from the end of the table and Mr Lloyd leapt up roaring, 'By God . . . By God, girl. We'll have no vegetarians here. Meat's my trade!' Here his voice accidentally slipped into a higher register and he had to bang the table to emphasise his words. 'Meat! Meat! Meat! Meat!' he squeaked.

Alun's restrained giggle went inwards and he snorted, piggily. Siôn choked on his orange juice and Iolo laughed out loud.

Nia hunched herself over the table, too close to the pink-tinged slice of meat. She couldn't foresee how it would all end, and then the doorbell rang, precipitating her into an even worse situation.

Somehow she knew the identity of their visitor even before her mother opened the front door, and when she heard Miss Oliver's shrill accusations her heart sank.

Mrs Lloyd called Nia into the hall. Her nose was twitching uncontrollably when she left the table and went to face the music.

'Why?'

'Why? Why? Why?' That was all the two women seemed capable of uttering.

And Nia couldn't reply. She couldn't explain why she had severed the beautiful creamy hem from the lace curtain.

The music teacher was in the hall now, her words

coming fast and hysterical. Her tight figure, a tiny rod of pent-up fury. She was literally hopping.

Mr Lloyd came out of the kitchen and the boys filled the open doorway behind him. Nerys spread her arms and blocked their passage. Catrin, anxious and bewildered, appeared beside her sister.

Nia backed to the stairs. Someone had told her to fetch the lace. Invisible mending had been mentioned. Punishments were suggested. Abject apologies were made. Nia knew all this though she scarcely heard the words through the dull ache in her head. And then she remembered something. She stood on the second stair and said, 'It was like trees!'

The three adults stared at her.

'What?' said Mr Lloyd at last. 'What did you say, girl?'

'Trees!' Nia repeated in a small voice. 'It was like blossom, you see. And I needed it!'

'Needed it?' Her father was roaring now.

More words, loud and angry, were coming at her like bullets and she fled up to her room. She took the lovely lace from her drawer and brushed it against her cheek. Even now, even when it was the cause of all the wrathful sounds beneath, she was reluctant to part with it. But she took it downstairs and held it out to Miss Oliver.

'What do you say, girl?' her father muttered.

'I say I'm sorry,' Nia said.

'And are you? Are you?' Miss Oliver's beetle eyebrows closed above her nose.

'Yes!' Nia murmured dutifully, and abandoned her parents to a task that was beyond her.

A phrase of her father's rose distinctly above the apologetic noises that she left behind; a description of herself. 'She's always been a problem but, I don't know

78

she seems to be getting worse . . . going up to that chapel
. . . cutting up new socks, we think . . . '

Nia closed her bedroom door and went to the window.
She watched the sparks in Morgan-the-Smithy's window.
She listened to his sons singing as though there was
nothing in the whole wide world to worry about.

She was not sorry for herself and regretted nothing but
the trouble she might have caused Catrin. She had
forgotten Catrin when she had cut Miss Oliver's lace,
forgotten that poor Catrin would have to face Miss Oliver
every week, remembering Nia's crime.

Nia opened her drawer and took out the tiny packet of
seeds: honesty, campion and poppy. She let them roll over
her palm while she remembered the garden at Tŷ Llŷr: the
brilliance of the poppies and the soft whiteness of the plum
trees in spring.

Later, when her mother came into the room, Nia was
still sitting on her bed, clasping the seeds.

Mrs Lloyd sat on Iolo's bed, facing her daughter. She
picked up Iolo's woolly blue monster and smoothed its
hair. She seemed to be waiting for a word to come from
somewhere to bring them closer but when that did not
happen, she got up and sat beside Nia on her bed. She was
breathing rather fast and the baby under her smock looked
very round and almost unreal. Nia was just wondering if
the baby would come soon when her mother asked, 'Is it
the baby, my love?'

'Baby?' Nia turned to her in surprise.

'Are you worried about us having another baby?'

'Oh no! I'm very pleased. I'm sure I'll like it,' Nia said,
as enthusiastically as she could.

'Is it Tŷ Llŷr then? Would you like to go back?'

'That's impossible.'

'No, it isn't, actually! We've had an idea, see. You know it's half term next week? Well, Alun's going to stay with Gwyn and Mrs Griffiths suggested that you should go too, and Iolo.'

Banished! But what a lucky banishment! 'Up to Tŷ Bryn?' Nia could scarcely believe it.

'Would you like that?'

'They don't mind?'

'Of course not. Mrs Griffiths asked specially; she wanted to help me out. I'm going to be so busy with Gareth and his leg when he comes home from hospital.'

Alun was a frequent overnight guest at the Griffiths' farmhouse, but Nia had never stayed. She had a sneaking feeling that it was her mother who had begged a favour, to keep her out of trouble. She did not care how the situation had come about. She would be going back to the mountain again. She could walk down to Tŷ Llŷr and care for her garden. 'What about punishment?' she asked. Surely life could not be so pleasant, not after what she had done.

'No pocket money for a month, your father says! We'll have to pay Mrs Bowen for invisible mending.' Mrs Lloyd sounded almost apologetic. 'And . . . and could you keep from being a vegetarian while you're with the Griffithses. We'll discuss it when you come home.'

'There's nothing to discuss, I just am one,' Nia said. 'But I can be tactful, you know!'

The lace was never mentioned again and Catrin, such a talented pianist and singer, was never reproached for her sister's crime. Prodigies are sensitive and Miss Oliver knew that any deterioration in her favourite pupil's performance would only reflect badly on herself.

6
Cold
Flowers

Mr Griffiths came to collect Alun, Nia and Iolo the following Saturday afternoon.

Iolo wanted to take two toy boxes, but having been persuaded that Gwyn would happily share his possessions, took only his blue monster.

Nia rolled her canvas in brown paper and tucked a small bag of scraps into a holdall that already contained a muddle of sweaters, socks and underwear.

'What've you got there girl? Not a rolling pin? My wife's fussy about her pastry!' Mr Griffiths laughed at his own joke as no one else seemed inclined to do so.

'It's my work,' Nia explained gravely. 'Something I have to do for school.'

'I see.' Mr Griffiths was a little disconcerted by Nia's sober expression. He was aware of her crime and hoped she wasn't going to be a problem.

Alun was already in the Landrover, chatting eagerly to Gwyn. He glanced resentfully at Nia and Iolo when they climbed in beside him. He had never had to share Gwyn with anyone, and regarded the Griffiths' home as his own, and a refuge from his siblings.

Left-behind Lloyds spilled out of the door on to the

81

pavement, waving and shouting instructions as the Landrover pulled away from the kerb, even Gareth with his plastered leg and Mr Lloyd in his striped butcher's apron and funny white hat. Nia wished her father had stayed indoors.

She had to take deep breaths in order to contain her excitement as the Landrover changed gear and began to ascend the hill out of Pendewi. And then they passed the chapel. She was sitting with her back to it, but she could not resist turning to look into the windows. There was no one there.

Mr Griffiths drove fast; he resented every minute away from his farm. Gwyn called his father 'demon-driver' and Nia wondered if the name implied talents other than fast driving. He had, after all, fathered a magician.

They were swinging up a familiar lane now. It rose steep and twisting between hedges sprinkled with hawthorn stars and green buds that would soon be honeysuckle. The windows were open and Nia inhaled the indescribable scent of new growth, of earth disturbed by movement and the sun. Beside the hedge golden celandine were opening and the brook glittered with melting mountain snow. There were crows and curlews tilting in the air and everywhere the great and mysterious rushing of bright grass towards the sky.

'There's Tŷ Llŷr!' Gwyn said.

'Tŷ Llŷr! Tŷ Llŷr!' shouted Iolo.

And Nia smiled, light-headed now and incapable of speech. She glimpsed white blossom, a deserted yard and two pigeons on a window sill. Later, she would come and leave a stale crust that Mrs Griffiths would surely give her.

They passed the white cottage where Gwyn's strange grandmother lived, with tall plants in every window and a

82

garden full of herbs. Round another bend and then the Landrover was bouncing off the lane and up the stone track beside Tŷ Bryn, a farmhouse much neater than Tŷ Llŷr; the porch freshly painted, the path free of weeds, and flowers beside the stone walls, confined in neat pebble-edged borders.

Gwyn's mother was waiting by the front door; a shy woman with soft brown hair and eyes to match. She never said much but she had always been kind. She took Iolo's bundle and would have taken both of Nia's, but Nia clung to her roll of canvas and said she was quite strong enough to carry her bag, thank you!

Inside the house, everywhere was clean and tidy, warm and bright. Wherever we live, us Lloyds, it will never be as neat as this, Nia thought. And yet this was where a magician lived.

Gwyn and Alun raced up two flights of stairs to Gwyn's attic room, where they would sleep side by side and share their private thoughts, once again.

Nia and Iolo followed Mrs Griffiths at a more respectful pace, Iolo chewing his monster's arm and looking apprehensive.

They were shown into a room where forget-me-not curtains fluttered in a window and three rag dolls with faded cheeks and button eyes sat on a white dressing-table. Dolls that looked as though they had been loved once but now were all forlorn because the person who had loved them had left them.

'It was my Bethan's room, Gwyn's sister, you know,' Mrs Griffiths explained, while Nia stared at the dolls.

Nia was to sleep in a bed covered in bright patchwork, Iolo on a mattress beside her.

'Can I go now?' said Iolo, more interested in the

outdoors than in bedrooms.

'Of course,' Mrs Griffiths smiled. 'I'll unpack your things, Iolo. We'll put your monster on the bed, shall we? There are white rabbits in the orchard.'

'Aww!' Iolo rushed out. He wouldn't leave his monster though.

'Are they wild?' Nia asked.

'Wild?' Mrs Griffiths looked confused.

'The rabbits!' Nia had a vision of Iolo chasing thistledown.

'Oh, no!' Mrs Griffiths laughed. 'They're in a hutch. We couldn't have them out and eating our lettuces, could we?'

'I suppose not,' Nia said solemnly. 'I'll unpack Iolo's

things. I'd like to.'

'Well, if you want.' Mrs Griffiths hesitated. 'I'll go back to my cooking. I'm not used to cooking for so many. I hope I get it right, cariad.'

Nia liked that. She liked the word 'cariad'. It made her feel at home. 'I expect you will,' she said, with a smile she had been told was the best part of her.

Quite unexpectedly Mrs Griffiths put her arms round Nia and hugged her quickly. 'It's good to have a girl in the house,' she said.

Nia, taken by surprise, murmured, 'I'll try . . . ' but did not know how to finish the sentence, and said instead, 'Could I go down to Tŷ Llŷr and see my garden?'

'Well, of course, cariad.' Mrs Griffiths, a neat plastic-aproned housewife again, rushed out. 'And visit Gwyn's Nain,' she called from the stairs. 'She'd be pleased to see you.'

Gwyn's grandmother doesn't know me, Nia thought. 'And I'm not going into that poky planty place alone,' she said to the rag dolls.

The dolls looked sympathetic. They watched Nia unpack her bag and open a drawer in the dressing-table. A dry sweet smell wafted out: roses! Nia opened the wardrobe. There were clothes inside: another girl's clothes; a yellow skirt, a grey coat and a blue dress with flowers on it. She began to remember someone: a girl with dark hair and eyes very like herself; a girl in a blue dress picking flowers in the lane. The wardrobe smelt of roses too.

Bethan's room softly enclosed her, settled smoothly and easily around her, as though she fitted exactly into a space in the dust that had been occupied, only a moment before, by someone else.

Nia unpacked Iolo's bag and began to lay his clothes in the second drawer, but seeing her reflection in the mirror, paused to loosen her long plaits of dark hair. The girl that now looked out at her belonged in a room with forget-me-not curtains, and the scent of roses. The rag dolls smiled with approval.

She closed the drawer, took one happy look around the room that was to be hers for a week, and went downstairs.

The boys were in the orchard, gathered round a pen where two white rabbits leapt enthusiastically about a pile of fresh dandelion leaves.

Fly bounded out of nowhere, greeting Nia with a display of delighted barking and rolling.

'I'm going to Tŷ Llŷr,' Nia called. She was glad no one responded. She wanted the place to herself. Fly was keen to accompany her though. 'Stay,' said Nia, rather too severely. 'You're Gwyn's dog now.'

She ran all the way, only slowing her pace when she passed Gwyn's grandmother in her garden. The old woman was leaning on a hoe, peering at a patch of earth.

'Bore da,' said Nia, knowing that the older Mrs Griffiths preferred to hear Welsh.

Mrs Griffiths looked up, her thoughts still with the patch of earth or whatever it was that should or should not be growing there. She wore a big straw hat squashed down over black curls. Her eyes could not be seen.

Receiving no reply to what she had considered a polite greeting, Nia ran on to Tŷ Llŷr. She didn't linger in the yard where the ghosts of hens gathered into awful emptiness. She didn't peep into the windows where rooms that she had known would be slowly dying. She ran straight to her wild garden by the stream – and received a great surprise.

Someone had been there. The earth round her poppies was brown and freshly turned; no weeds to strangle the orange gold flowers. And how they had flourished! Divided and replanted they covered the ground in huge brilliant clusters.

'Oh!' Nia cried. 'Who did it?'

Beyond the poppies where thick rushes crept up the bank, someone had built a low stone wall, three layers deep, to keep the weeds at bay, and here and there blue forget-me-nots grew, like tiny pieces of reflected sky.

There was nothing for Nia to do but sit beside her flowers and watch the water.

'I'll forget the church and those old yews,' she muttered, thinking of her canvas, 'and I'll make Tŷ Llŷr and my garden.' She wondered if she could persuade Mrs Griffiths to find yellow cloth. She had a feeling she would be offered a duster.

Happier now, and confident, she walked back to the house and risked a quick peep in her old home. She chose a window overhung with the blossom of two ancient plum trees that curved towards each other from either side. Ghosts of absent furniture stood against the walls; pale shapes on the stained and lived-in wallpaper: a cupboard, a dresser, a silent piano. The only three-dimensional furnishing now was a neat pile of torn paper in a corner. Home for a mouse!

As she stepped away from the window she almost trod on the soldier: a small knitted soldier with a red coat, a stripe of yellow buttons and a tall black hat. Not a Lloyd toy; she knew every one of those. Nia slipped the soldier into her pocket.

The two wood pigeons, bold as brass, were pecking in the yard. If Mr Butcher Lloyd had been there, he would have run for his gun. 'Wood pigeons are a pest,' he would say. 'They'll get my seed.' If Mr Lloyd had been there, the pigeons would have left. But this year they would nest in the sycamore tree and there might be four or five pigeons living at Tŷ Llŷr. Nia wished she had remembered the crust.

She wandered out of the yard, closing the big gate out of habit, though now there was no reason to do so.

Nain Griffiths was standing by her garden wall when Nia passed, as though she had been waiting. She was wearing a purple cardigan so bright it was almost shouting and there were pearly pink parrots swinging from her ears.

'Hello!' said Nia, over the wall.

'Bore da, Nia,' returned Gwyn's grandmother.

'You know?' said Nia, astonished.

'I know my neighbours, don't I?' said old Mrs Griffiths.

'But you knew which one I was; you knew I was Nia. Nobody ever knows me, I'm in the middle, see!'

'Well, I know you, don't I?' The dark and wrinkled face came closer; pink birds quivering under grey-black curls. 'I don't know any of the others, but I know you!'

'Oh!' Nia stepped back, but not to be outdone she asked, 'Have you been weeding my garden?'

'Weeding?'

'Yes. I've got poppies by the stream and someone has been caring for them, doing some gardening there. Was it you?'

'Don't you think I've got enough to do?' Gwyn's grandmother heaved a forkful of stringy weeds above the gate. A shower of mud and leaves flew into the air, some landing on Nia's head.

'Sorry!' said Nia. 'It was just a guess.' It was not she who should have apologized she thought, but it was quite evident that old Mrs Griffiths did not regret showering her with mud. Nia began to run up the lane.

'Pob hwyl!' Nain Griffiths called after her. 'Come and see me soon.'

'Same to you!' Nia shouted without turning. She didn't think she would call on Gwyn's grandmother again, if she could help it.

After lunch, which was shepherd's pie and much better than Nia expected, the boys announced that they were going to walk up the mountain.

'And what about Nia?' Mr Griffiths could have been smiling under his heavy moustache, it was difficult to tell.

'I might, that is I . . . ' Nia hesitated.

'Going to help muck out the hens, are you, then?'

'Well . . . ' Nia began. 'Someone's been in the garden at Tŷ Llŷr,' she said changing the subject. 'Caring for my plants; building a little wall an' that.'

Mr Griffiths gaped speechlessly at Nia. It was as if she had said there were wolves in the wood.

Mrs Griffiths was washing up. She didn't see her husband's face. 'I'm afraid I've no time for other people's gardens,' she said. 'Perhaps it was Nain?'

'No,' said Nia. 'I asked her.' She was fascinated by Mr Griffiths' discomfort.

Shifting away from Nia's disturbing scrutiny, Mr Griffiths left the kitchen without a word and went out into the yard.

'Perhaps it was Gwyn?' Nia persisted.

'Gwyn's no gardener,' Mrs Griffiths replied. 'His sister was though!' She suddenly dropped a pan and became quite still, her shoulders hunched and her hands motionless in the soapy water. Nia couldn't see her expression, but her voice changed pitch and she said,

89

'Why don't you run along now and follow the boys.'

Nia went. Why had her garden caused such a stir?

The boys were wandering up the mountain track, surrounded by ewes and their fat, excitable lambs. The air was full of noisy bleating; Iolo was happily echoing the sounds; he'd abandoned his woolly monster at last.

Nia did not catch up with the boys; she did not intend to. They passed the stone wall where the track rose away from the field and disappeared from sight.

Nia left the track and walked on through the field. She could hear the boys above her, climbing now and shouting to each other.

Nia was in Griffiths' land, but she knew it well. The mountain had belonged to her mother's family, the Llŷrs, and their sheep, for as long as anyone could remember. Her feet fitted well into the hard slanting land. She wandered south, towards the sun, while the voices above her became lost in the chorus of sheep and streams.

She had been walking for a mile up and down, still in the same landscape, when she came upon a place she could not remember: a valley lay below her, where blossom floated like a cloud among darker trees; an orchard of palest pink apple blossom swept like a crescent moon round a low cottage with a mossy green roof and smoke drifting from the chimney. Perhaps she had never been there in spring; never looked down into the valley; it was the blossom that had made her look.

Nia began to walk down into the trees. The ground became steeper and she was suddenly precipitated into a rushing, sliding descent. Breathless and frightened she caught hold of a branch and saw a path, narrow but well-trodden, that wound between the trees. Someone often came this way. But there was no place for a car or a vehicle of any kind.

On the path her pace became more dignified. She had
time to observe the land before her. The wood was
ancient: oak and ash trees, their branches dappled with the
pale green of leaves not fully grown; delicate rowan and
bushy hazel and, now and then, a holly tree, shining dark
and dangerous in the distance. And then Nia was in the
orchard. The sun was high, sparkling through the bright
canopy of blossom. But Nia was cold! She was walking

91

through flowers; tall and dense they covered the ground beneath the apple trees. They were white flowers, huge blooms, like stars on tall stems; their leaves broad spears of emerald.

Nia bent to pick a flower and gasped; it was like touching ice!

7
A Visit
to Nain
Griffiths

Holding the flower cautiously by the stem, Nia moved through the orchard. The cold began to penetrate her shoes and socks, it moved up her body and she began to shiver. She might have been walking through a field of snow.

She emerged from the orchard and came into a garden where the low cottage stood surrounded by wild flowers. It seemed to be utterly deserted. Lost. The silence was profound. Yet smoke still drifted from the chimney.

All at once Nia became aware that she was trespassing; that this was a very secret and private place. She turned back into the orchard and began to run. She ran from the silence and the cold white flowers.

Stumbling over brambles and loose rocks that seemed, suddenly, to have invaded the well-trodden path, Nia began to make her way out of the valley. The valley, it appeared, was reluctant to let her go. It tried to halt her progress with stones that slid beneath her feet, with wet and slippery stalks, twigs that caught in her loose hair and thorns that scratched her face. She threaded the white flower into her hair, freeing her hands to protect her face. The ground was surely steeper than it had been on her descent. Nia began to panic. She could see a misty rim of trees at the top of the valley and climbed towards them, but in doing so lost the path. The quiet wood closed in upon her, a damp blanket of decaying leaves smothered her feet and, tired and uncertain, she stopped moving. 'Nerys would say a poem,' she muttered aloud. 'Catrin would sing! But Nia-can't-do-nothing. Nia is trapped!'

'Nia *can* do something!' admonished Idris Llewelyn who had assumed the shape of a broad oak.

Pulling her feet through the leaves, Nia ran towards a bank and climbed upwards, hand over hand, until she burst through bushes of sweet-smelling elderflower, and fell into a field where sheep stared anxiously at her sudden and violent arrival.

'All right, so I was scared,' Nia said to her audience, 'but I didn't notice any of *you* down there!'

The sheep regarded her, unblinking. A few spoke back, and then they frightened themselves into a wild and disorganized retreat.

'Who's scared now?' Nia called after them and laughed. She felt safe out in the rough sunlit field, and ran happily, all the way back to the farmhouse.

The boys were already there. Their muddy boots were in the porch.

'They're up in Gwyn's room!' Mrs Griffiths told Nia.

She climbed the stairs quickly, reluctant to intrude on male territory but eager to discuss her adventure.

'Where've you been?' Alun asked suspiciously when Nia walked in on them. 'We called and called!'

'Just walking,' she replied. 'I haven't done nothing that I shouldn't've!'

Alun looked relieved. 'Gwyn's rabbits are expecting,' he said. 'We can have some of the babies and keep them in a hutch out in the yard at Number 6.'

'Dad would kill them!' The words spilled out; she still resented Alun's first question.

The boys looked appalled.

'He never . . . ' Alun said at last.

'He would!' Nia couldn't stop herself. 'It's his trade now. He'd chop off their heads and hang them in his window.'

'You're mean, Nia,' Iolo cried. 'Our dad 'ud never kill white rabbits. They'd be ours; our pets!'

'What's that?' Gwyn was staring at the white flower, hanging in Nia's hair. She had forgotten it.

'I found it in a valley,' she said, 'a valley I never noticed before, with an orchard and a stone cottage.'

Gwyn came over and took the flower out of her hair. No one but Nia heard his quiet gasp as he touched it. 'It's cold,' he said.

'And it shines,' Alun remarked. 'It's like those luminous stars on your watch, Gwyn.'

Gwyn cupped his hands round the starlike petals. He gazed at the flower, saying nothing. The others looked down into the dark cradle of Gwyn's hands. Each petal glowed like a Christmas-tree lantern.

'Awww!' Iolo exclaimed. 'It's beeee-autiful!'

'There are lots of them in the valley,' Nia said. 'Thousands. Can I have it now?'

Gwyn held the flower out to her. 'There are some in our garden too,' he said thoughtfully. 'But they're not so big and they don't shine. My sister planted them.'

Mrs Griffiths called them to tea and they tumbled out of Gwyn's attic room, down the twelve ladder steps that led from it, across the narrow landing and then on down the conventional and carpeted staircase. The mountain air

95

had made them hungry.

They crowded expectantly round the long kitchen table where plates of fruit cake and sandwiches had been laid on a white cloth.

'May I have a glass?' Nia asked Mrs Griffiths. 'It's for my flower. Look!'

'Well, well I never! It's beautiful, Nia. Where did you find it?'

'In a valley,' Nia replied, 'with an orchard and a little cottage. There were hundreds of them.'

Mr Griffiths, already drinking tea at the table, looked up. 'I wouldn't go there, girl!' he said sternly.

'Why not?' Nia couldn't stop herself.

'Because I say not, that's why!' Gwyn's father barked out.

The children, subdued, sat down and began their tea.

Mrs Griffiths put Nia's flower in a tall glass and placed it on the table, but after the meal Nia took it up to her room and stood it on the dressing-table beside the rag dolls. They brightened in its presence, as though the dust of four years had been swept off their raggedy faces and pretty cotton clothes.

The Griffiths family went early to bed. Nia lay in her new room listening to Gwyn's parents moving about on the other side of the passage. She heard Gwyn and Alun murmuring in their attic. Iolo fell asleep on his mattress beside her.

Nia couldn't close her eyes. The pale flower glowed in the dark, its reflection in the mirror sent points of light dancing into the room. Why were so many places forbidden? First the Llewelyn's chapel, now the orchard valley, and it all came back to solitary, taciturn Mr Griffiths.

Wide awake, she crept to the window and drew back the forget-me-not curtains. The round shadow of the earth almost obliterated the moon, only a tiny slither was left, hanging like a sickle among the myriads of distant stars.

Nia turned on her bedside light. Undisturbed, Iolo slept soundly in shadow on the other side of her bed. She took her canvas from a rose-scented drawer and rolled it out. One corner insisted on curling upwards so she set the rag dolls on the offending place and spread glue across the top of the canvas. She took a length of dark blue velvet from her rag-bag, cut it to shape and pressed it on to the glue. A midnight sky! She dotted the velvet with glue and shook Christmas glitter on to the dots. The glitter clustered in bright constellations, just as she wanted. Bethan's dolls looked on with interest.

Nia worked well. She cut green for the grass, violet, black and brown for the trees and their shadows, and grey for the drystone walls; purple for foxgloves and yellow for buttercups, but there was nothing in her bag that would do for her special orange-gold poppies.

When she turned off her light and climbed into bed, the multicoloured cockerel was crowing from his roost.

Nia tackled the problem of the poppies after breakfast next morning. Mrs Griffiths was kneading dough on the kitchen table.

'Have you got a piece of cloth, orangey-gold, like the poppies at Tŷ Llŷr?'

'What for, cariad?'

'My work,' Nia replied. She felt it unnecessary to give any more information.

'I see,' Mrs Griffiths seemed to find Nia's answer adequate. She rinsed her floury fingers under the tap and went to a cupboard.

'There's all sorts in here.' She pulled out a large box and set it on the kitchen table. The box was stuffed with pieces of torn shirts, holey socks and even underwear. Mrs Griffiths held up a faded T-shirt.

Nia shook her head. 'It has to be like the poppies.'

'Well, that's all there is. You could dye something, I suppose. Go and see Gwyn's grandmother; she knows all about dye, she does it with flowers and herbs.'

'No. I don't want to go there, thanks!'

'Why ever not!' Mrs Griffiths seemed disconcerted by Nia's candour.

'She's peculiar-like, isn't she? Gwyn's Nain? And I don't fancy going in that dark old place with all those plants poking in at me.'

Mrs Griffiths laughed. 'What a girl you are, Nia Lloyd!' She went to the door and called, 'Gwyn, come here. I want you to take Nia down to see Nain.'

Gwyn came rattling down the stairs. Alun and Iolo followed, less enthusiastically

'What's it about?' Gwyn asked.

Mrs Griffiths put the T-shirt into Nia's hands. 'Nia has to dye something. Nain will show her how.'

'Aw heck,' moaned Alun. 'We don't have to go, do we?'

'I don't want to,' Iolo added nervously, from behind his brother.

'There'd be no room in there for you two, anyway,' Gwyn assured him. 'We won't be long.' He was about to rush out of the front door when he suddenly stopped and said to Nia, 'Bring the flower!'

Grateful, Nia ran up to the bedroom and took the white flower out of the glass. Was it her imagination, or had the flower grown in the night? She took it downstairs and gave

98

it to Gwyn. He frowned at it, puzzled, and then said, 'Come on!'

They left Alun and Iolo in the lane, playing with Fly. The young sheep-dog seemed to have forgotten her nightmare at Number 6. Her barks were joyful here. Nia thought of Emlyn.

But Gwyn had other things on his mind. He was staring at the flower, gingerly touching the icy petals with his forefinger.

They walked in silence until they reached a white gate with the name 'Coed Melyn' – the yellow wood – painted in green upon it.

Nia stopped, twisting the T-shirt in her hands.

'She won't bite!' Gwyn grinned.

'Won't she?' Nia followed Gwyn through the gate and up a cinder path bordered with tall, fragrant flowers. The door was opened before they had reached it and Gwyn's grandmother stood on her step, dressed all in red, with a gold belt round her waist and rings on every finger.

'Has your prince come then, Nain?' Gwyn asked his grandmother.

'Not yet! Not yet!' The old woman giggled at their private joke. 'Who's this, then?' She poked a finger at Nia.

'You know who I am!' Nia said fiercely. 'You said you knew.'

'Just testing!' Nain Griffiths laid her ringed fingers on Nia's arm and drew her into the room beyond.

It was not as bad as Nia expected. Dark, yes, but colourful, and the plants that lived there jostled with ropes of beads, painted pottery, ancient jewelled boxes, ostrich feathers and exotic shawls. You could hardly see the furniture beneath. Such splendours could not be

99

appreciated by a quick peep through a window, and that was all that Nia had ventured until today.

'Take a seat and I'll bring you rosehip syrup,' Nain commanded and disappeared behind a screen.

The only seats were patchwork cushions on the floor. A black hen slept in the armchair. The children sat down, and Nia found she had settled beside a white cat in a glass box. Her nose began its nervous twitching.

Nain Griffiths reappeared and gave the children mugs of warm rosy liquid. Nia sipped suspiciously, but it was very good.

'Look at this, Nain,' Gwyn said, offering her the white flower. 'Feel the petals!'

Nain Griffiths took the flower. She sniffed it, touched it, gasped and regarded it with her head on one side, as though listening for a message from the ground. 'Well, I don't know,' she murmured. 'It's not of this earth, child. It doesn't belong here!' and she darted a look at Gwyn, so fierce and full of meaning, Nia was quite shaken.

'What is it?' she asked.

They looked at her, Gwyn and his grandmother and then Gwyn said, 'Two years ago my sister came back. I called her with . . . ' he hesitated, looked at his hands and then at his grandmother who nodded approvingly, '. . . with the power I inherited from my ancestors.'

'From the dead?' Nia whispered.

'She's not dead!' Gwyn's black eyes were fathomless. 'She's out there.' He looked towards chinks of sky behind red flowers in the window; somehow Nia knew that he meant to indicate a place beyond the sky. 'They took her,' he went on, 'things that look like children but aren't human. Icy things that smile and sing and make you want to be with them. Bethan wanted to go and they took her.
100

She's happy there, she said.'

'Where?' Nia's throat was dry and the question came out in a frightened croak.

'On a planet of ice, where everything is covered in snow. She'd changed her name and she was cold and pale, even the colour in her eyes had been washed away.'

'How did you call her?' Nia found a small tight voice. Gwyn seemed to have brought frost into the room.

'I had her scarf,' he smiled slyly, the way a wizard might, 'and I gave it to the wind. Do you know about Gwydion, the magician, and the seaweed?'

'He made a ship,' she said, and because she almost knew what Gwyn was going to tell her, added, 'out of seaweed.'

'Gwydion lived in these mountains,' Gwyn said. 'Sometimes I think he's still here inside me.' He looked at his fingers; long, sinewy fingers, too long for a boy. 'Nain gave me seaweed for my birthday.' He glanced at his grandmother, tall and crimson, her eyes fixed on her grandson, reliving with him the moment when the strange inherited power had awakened in him. 'I threw my seaweed from the mountain and a ship fell out of space. It was silver and there were icicles clinging to it. The cold of it hurt my eyes, hurt all of me and I could barely see. It brought my sister back.'

Nia stared at Gwyn and at his young-old hands. She had seen his power in the churchyard. 'Where is Bethan now?' she asked softly.

'She went back.'

'How?'

'On the ship. Alun knows.'

'Alun?' How had Alun managed to keep a secret like that? And then Nia remembered the time he had been lost

101

in snow on the mountain but had miraculously survived. Gwyn had saved him, somehow, with the power that no one believed in. 'At school they teased you,' she said.

'Children are cruel,' Nain muttered, 'when they don't believe.'

Nia had no such difficulty. 'It was very cold the day we moved from Tŷ Llŷr,' she went on. 'It came suddenly. Was it the ship? Did you call your sister again?'

'No. I didn't call. There's something I don't understand,' said Gwyn. 'Perhaps it has to do with the flower.'

Nain brought the flower close to her face. Shadows appeared on her strange, lined features. She was beautiful, Nia realised, in a way that rocks and trees and ancient polished things were beautiful.

They sipped their sweet drink for a while and then Nia said, 'You used your power on Emlyn Llewelyn.'

'What?' said Nain Griffiths. 'What's this I hear, Gwydion Gwyn? Did you abuse your power, then?'

'No, Nain,' Gwyn cried. 'I never hurt him. I had to stop him for a while. He was angry, unreasonable.' And he told Nain about Nia and Fly, about the dog's lead and the fight in the churchyard. 'But I let him win, Nain,' he finished. 'I knew I had to do that!'

'That may be,' said Nain, 'but it's not right what your father and the town have done to Emlyn Llewelyn.'

Nia had never heard anyone put Emlyn's point of view. 'Why?' she asked.

'They're ignorant,' Nain said scathingly. 'Idris Llewelyn is an artist, trying to do his best, making things beautiful. And there is his wife, Gwyn's aunt, leaving her husband and her own boy just because she hasn't got electricity!'

102

Gwyn jumped up. 'She couldn't live in that old chapel. She wanted a proper home for her baby. Uncle Idris was cruel and wicked, Dad says.'

'Emlyn stayed,' Nia said quietly.

'He should have gone with his mam, he should!' Gwyn retorted.

'Emlyn stayed because he knows what's right He's loyal and he's brave and you and he should be friends, Gwydion Gwyn, and not fighting in a sacred place, where you know the power is all on your side!' Nain's tone was not unkind but Gwyn turned from her resentfully as she passed him and whisked the T-shirt out of Nia's hands. 'Now let us see what we can do with this!' she said.

'How did you know?' asked Nia, astonished.

'I can't imagine you would visit me just for pleasure, Nia Loyd,' Nain teased.

Nia did not answer that question. 'I wanted to make some orange cloth,' she confessed. 'It's for my work. I want to make it the colour of Welsh poppies – my own special poppies by the stream at Tŷ Llŷr. Gwyn's mam said you could do it.'

Nain beckoned Nia out behind the yellow screen into her kitchen. Nia followed cautiously. She watched Nain Griffiths take a large enamel pot from the wall, fill it with water and set it on her stove. 'First, onion skins,' Nain muttered and pulled six onions from a neatly plaited string hanging from the low-beamed ceiling. 'Peel them!' she commanded, handing Nia the onions.

Nia put them on the table and began to dig her nails into the crackling skins; her eyes smarted and as she looked up to wipe the tears away, she heard the front door bang and Gwyn's footsteps running up the lane.

'Don't cry,' Nain Griffiths chuckled. 'He's a sensitive

103

boy but he'll come round. And you needn't be afraid of me!'

'It's the onions,' said Nia, annoyed by the tears. 'And I'm not afraid.'

The hours that then sped by seemed more like five minutes. Nia stood by while Gwyn's grandmother stirred a boiling liquid of onion skins and lichen until it turned golden. Into this bubbling, syrupy water she dropped the faded T-shirt which had first been washed by Nia in the sink. They then took turns with the stirring, using a wooden spoon as long as Nia's arm, and while they stirred Nain told Nia about the boy who had just left them. About the line of magic that stretched back through her family to a time when princes and magicians ruled Wales, and the people that Nia had thought were only part of a story became as real to her as the mountain beyond Nain's door. She saw a time and place where enchantment was a necessity, the life-blood of an ancient people, who had changed and grown through invasion and suppression, still keeping a small piece of magic inside themselves until, once every century perhaps, it bubbled out and a witch was burned or driven to secrecy, like Gwyn Griffiths.

'And you have it, too, Nia Lloyd!' said Nain, breaking into Nia's thoughts.

'Me?' she exclaimed, amazed. 'But I'm no one. I'm in the middle. I can't do nothing!'

'What's this, then?' Nain lifted a spoonful of golden liquid and let it trickle back into the pot. 'Turning white cloth to gold, isn't it? And aren't you a Llŷr, whose ancestors once ruled Britain. There's a little bit of power left inside you, Nia Lloyd, if you look for it!'

The shirt was pulled out and hung, steaming from the huge spoon, darker by several shades. It was thrust under cold water, squeezed and put on the stove to dry, while Nain and Nia nibbled biscuits made of oats and berries.

'You'll have to leave the cloth with me for a day or two, for the dye to set,' Nain told Nia. 'But you'll come again, won't you, if you need more colours?'

'Oh, I will,' Nia replied fervently.

When she left Coed Melyn she was older by far more than a few hours. And she was stronger, strong enough, perhaps, to bring together two boys who had been divided by a silly quarrel that had nothing to do with them.

8

The
Wrong
Reflection

Nia kept her own company for the rest of the holiday. She did not mention Emlyn again. The days were warm and dry; days for the boys to help with fence-mending, stone-wall building and sheep dipping, and for playing barefoot in the streams when their work was done.

Nia was excused farm duties and allowed to work in Bethan's room. Through the open window the boys' cheerful voices were companionable and undemanding. She worked well. The canvas began to come to life.

Nain Griffiths came to the house one day, holding a piece of bright cloth, as gloriously golden-orange as a bouquet of poppies. And that night Nia cut her poppies to shape and sewed them neatly in place, beside a stream of silver tinsel and blue forget-me-nots that had once been Mrs Bowen's satin underwear.

By the end of the week Nia had recovered her confidence sufficiently to believe that she could, after all, visit the Llewelyns again. She would say she had come to fetch the violet dress and Mr Llewelyn would welcome her in and finish her portrait. Emlyn would have to forgive her.

Happily absorbed in future plans, Nia left Tŷ Bryn believing that her canvas could be a masterpiece; and that her friendship with Emlyn would surely be renewed.

As she said 'goodbye' to Mrs Griffiths she told her, 'It's the best holiday I ever had, anywhere!' And she meant it.

Mrs Griffiths seemed sad at their departure. 'We don't see enough of girls up here,' she said wistfully. 'Come again, cariad!'

'If you'll have me,' Nia beamed.

Gwyn was nowhere to be seen. She hoped he didn't regret the secrets he had confided.

Nain Griffiths was standing by her gate when the Landrover bounced past. She was wearing a dress she had dipped in the bowl of Nia's poppy-gold dye. She did a little dance and blew a kiss. Nia had to laugh. She knelt on the seat and leant out of the window. 'You're a poppy!' she cried, and waved until the bright figure was out of sight.

'She's batty, Gwyn's grandmother!' Alun remarked.

'She's not! She's fantastic!' Nia leapt down and glared at Alun. 'I think she's a great lady, would have been a queen, probably, if the Anglo-Saxons hadn't come, and all that lot!'

All at once Mr Griffiths began to roar with laughter. He couldn't stop. It was such an unusual sound to come from him; the children stared at his shaking back in perplexity and Alun couldn't decide who was the most mad, his sister or his best friend's relations.

Number 6 seemed unbearably dark and muddled after the clear mountain light. There were sheets and shirts mounded on chairs, waiting to be ironed. Stained butcher's aprons were piled by the washing-machine. Gareth, with his autographed white leg, was, somehow, everywhere, moaning because he 'couldn't sit down nowhere!' He'd tried putting his foot on a chair and smashed a lens in Nerys's spectacles.

107

Nerys was in a horrendous mood. Her new hairdo had gone wrong: mousy spikes framed her long face and she regarded everything with a slit-eyed furious glance. Siôn was fed up with Gareth's moaning and even calm Catrin was thumping out Mozart like she was massaging a footballer.

Nia had brought her white flower, the stem wrapped carefully in damp tissue. To save bothering her mother she put the flower in her blue tooth-mug and set it on the window sill. It looked as bright and as fresh as ever.

Mrs Lloyd had forgotten that she would have three extra for tea and it was Sunday, so she couldn't run to the shops.

'I don't need cake,' Nia informed them. 'I want to go and see Gwyneth. I've got to ask her something about school. Can I go now?'

'Well, seeing as it's about school . . . !' Mrs Lloyd gratefully cut the remaining piece of fruit cake into eight neat slices.

Nia squeezed between the dresser and her brothers on their bench, happily relinquishing fruit cake in order to escape.

'Won't be long!' she called confidently from the hall.

Outside she did not feel so sure of herself. The walk up to the chapel seemed longer than usual, but she did not have to knock. Idris Llewelyn was painting silver leaves beneath the gold flowers on his door. 'I hadn't finished,' he told Nia, 'but it's done now. Do you approve?'

Nia nodded and followed him into the chapel. Emlyn was sitting on the floor with a book; he did not look at her.

'Well, get up, boy, and welcome your visitor,' said Mr Llewelyn. He prodded his son gently with a sandalled foot. 'Had a bit of trouble with you, Nia, and his cousin, I heard: about the dog!'

'It wasn't my fault,' Nia blurted out. 'Dad sold it to Mr Griffiths. I tried to stop him. But I couldn't . . . couldn't tell you. I was a coward!'

'Not a coward, just cautious. And Emlyn is contrite! Aren't you, boy? He came to see you in the holiday.'

'Did you?' Nia looked at Emlyn in surprise. She perched herself on a cushion beside him, but he still refused to respond. He hasn't forgiven me; he never will, she thought.

'You weren't there,' he said at last, and still without looking at her. 'That sister of yours opened the door. The one with specs. I'm sorry but I can't stand her.'

'I know what you mean,' Nia said. Now and again there were good reasons for being disloyal. 'Did she say something spiteful? They didn't want me to come here again. They sent me away, up to Gwyn Griffiths' place, with Alun and Iolo. I'd been in trouble, see!'

'Trouble?' Mr Llewelyn sounded concerned.

'I thought everyone would know by now. Miss Olwen Oliver is famous for her gossip.'

'We haven't seen no one,' Emlyn murmured. 'No one comes here.'

'Tell us your trouble, girl.' Mr Llewelyn put his silvery brush into a jar of spirit and sat on an extraordinarily large upturned bucket.

'The first thing was,' Nia began, 'I said I was a vegetarian.'

Emlyn looked up.

'Well that didn't go down too well, Dad being a butcher. The next thing happened because I wanted something for blossom and I couldn't think what, so I . . . so I . . .'

'Go on,' Emlyn said, with a spark of interest.

'So I cut a piece of lace from Miss Olwen Oliver's curtain. I did that before being a vegetarian, but they didn't know,' Nia said in a rush. 'I didn't think it would notice, well, it *didn't* notice, but she saw, didn't she? And, aw heck, there was so much trouble.' She sighed and rolled her eyes towards the ceiling, remembering the horror of it all.

When she dared to observe the effect her confession had made, she found that Mr Llewelyn's very white teeth were showing through the mass of brown hair on his face. He was smiling, and then he was laughing, and Emlyn with him.

'But it was a terrible thing I did,' Nia reproached them.

'It was! It was!' agreed Mr Llewelyn. 'Excuse us! Why didn't you come to us, cariad bach? We can give you lace and anything you need for your masterpiece.' He strode to a wooden box beneath one of the long windows and flung it open. 'Look!' he exclaimed. 'Lace and cotton, feathers and pretty things!' He held up a dress, the palest of pink cotton embossed with white flowers. 'Blossom! Don't you agree?'

The children stood, simultaneously. Emlyn was staring at his father and at the dress.

'What d'you think, Emlyn? Shall I give this to Nia for her work?' His words were somehow more than a question. Nia had the feeling that, perhaps, he was trying to lay a ghost.

Emlyn was still gazing at the dress. He screwed up his face, like someone with toothache. 'I don't mind,' he said at last.

'No anorak to hide it in today,' observed Mr Llewelyn. 'Will you dare to say you got the dress from us?'

'I'll say it was from Gwyneth Bowen. I'm always getting

wool and stuff out of her mam's shop. They'll believe me.'

'Nia Lloyd, you have criminal tendencies,' Idris Llewelyn remarked, with half a smile.

'No, I never . . . ' she began, but the big man laughed again and bundled the dress into her arms.

'Will you stay for tea?' he asked.

Nia hesitated. She dared not risk trouble on her first day at home. 'I'll come tomorrow,' she said.

When she left, Emlyn followed her out on to the road but no further. He sat on the chapel steps and when she turned back to wave he would not look at her; his chin was cupped in his hands and he was staring out at distant, empty mountains.

He hasn't forgiven me, Nia thought. But he will, he must!

Everything at Number 6 had simmered down, by the time Nia returned. The boys were by the river examining something dead on the bank, while the three big Morgan brothers shouted fishy information across the water. The river was low and so was the sun. The water sparkled gold over smooth stones and bare feet.

'What's that?' Iolo poked a wet finger at the dress in Nia's arms.

'Don't!' she sprang back. 'It's for my work.'

'Oh!' He fished a handkerchief from his pocket and a matchbox came tumbling out and fell into a shallow pool at his feet. 'Aw, no!' he cried, retrieving the damp box. 'Nia, take it inside for me, will you?'

'What is it?'

'A spider! I found it at Gwyn's place. It's special, like silver!'

Nia took the box and left them to decide the identity of the dead fish. She passed the window of her father's 'cold

111

room'; told herself not to look in, but did. The sight was even more gory than she had imagined. Her father was removing unimaginable things from something lying on a bloody slab – and he was whistling!

She ran up to her room where curiosity prompted her to open Iolo's matchbox. The spider was, indeed, special: very tiny, silvery and, like the white flower, it seemed to glow.

She put the box on the chest of drawers, slightly open so that the spider could breath or spin, or do anything a spider should do.

The boys would be in the river for hours, she could tell. There was no one to bother her. She knelt down and spread the dress on the floor. It was almost too beautiful to

112

cut but someone had already done that. The hem had been unevenly severed, slashed, hastily, as though with a knife.

The sight was, somehow, rather shocking. Nia scissored away the painful gashes, neatening the wound, tidying the sad, pale dress. She put the severed strands into a rag-bag and then, almost by accident, found herself slipping the dress over her head. The cuffs of the long full sleeves covered her fingers, the high collar tickled her neck, very softly.

She smoothed the dress close to her body, over her skirt and crumpled shirt. It concealed everything but her trainers. Elinor Llewelyn must have been tall and slim.

Nia wished she could see herself. A mirror had been promised once. Catrin and Nerys had a mirror in their room that reached to the ground, but Nerys was probably there reading.

Sometimes a hint of a reflection would emerge from the wardrobe's shiny doors. Today, to Nia's amazement, there was more than a hint. A huge circle of shimmering silver hung over the doors: a cobweb, spun so fine, so close, that it resembled a mirror. How it had come there, and when, Nia could not imagine but it must have been the work of Iolo's spider for there it was, at the very top, swinging on an inch of gossamer.

The window was open and the web was blown into a slow, deep movement, like a wave. Nia waited for it to calm. She could already see the pink dress and dark hair above it, like someone lying under clear water. Gradually, features began to appear, large dark eyes, a pale face and lips, parted in a scream. The face that looked out at Nia was not hers

Nia screamed, and went on screaming. She gasped for air, terrified and trembling.

'Nia, what is it?' Catrin stood behind her, clasping her shoulders.

'Not me! It's not me!' sobbed Nia. 'Not my face!' She pointed to where a dark woman's features had replaced her own, but the shining cobweb had broken loose. A cloud of silvery threads streamed out towards them, and drifted through the open window.

9

Children after Midnight

Later, when Nia had recovered and Mam sat reading by her bed, the spider crawled over the carved pattern at the top of the wardrobe. The tiny creature mesmerized her, but when her mother anxiously inquired whether Nia was 'seeing things' again, she replied, 'It's nothing. I was thinking!'

They had not understood, of course, and Nia had no intention of trying to explain what she had seen. Her scream had not been a call for help. It had just burst out of her at the sight of something unnatural. She had experienced the same sensation in the churchyard, when Gwyn Griffiths had interrupted time, but he'd stolen her breath as well so she had not been able to cry out.

Was it coincidence that her mother was reading of Welsh magicians; magicians who had also been soldiers, kings and princes. Could Gwyn bring them, even here, in safely terraced Number 6?

She did not doubt that Gwyn was responsible for the mysterious cobweb, and for the spider that was now moving so gracefully over carved wooden flowers. Mrs Lloyd's quiet voice drifted on, soothing herself as well as her children. She seemed almost to be talking to the baby inside her, Nia thought.

The white flower on the window sill began to glow as the sky behind it deepened into a gloomy twilight. Iolo fell asleep. He couldn't see the spider he had taken from Gwyn Griffiths, hadn't seen the magic he had stolen.

'Nos da, cariad,' Mrs Lloyd bent and kissed her daughter.

'Good night, Mam!'

'Better now?'

'Yes, Mam. I'm sorry to be a nuisance.'

'You can go back to Tŷ Llŷr again, you know, for a visit. It isn't far.'

'No, Mam.' Nia smiled and closed her eyes. She had just had a wonderful idea.

Her mother drew the curtains, carefully moving the flower as she did so. 'Trust you to find a strange plant,' she muttered. 'Never seen anything like it.'

After school next day, Nia left Gwyneth Bowen at the school gates, the latter still half-way through a recital of her hamster's holiday misadventures.

'You are rude, Nia Lloyd,' Gwyneth called after her. 'You don't care about animals, do you? You don't care if Gethin put my Sandy in the freezer, do you? You're callous, you are!'

'So's Gethin,' Nia shouted back. She had spied Emlyn Llewelyn striding up through the town, always the first to leave school.

Nia tore after him, twisting herself into her back-pack and her jacket. She gave up trying to wear them and carried them in a bundle before her.

'Hold on! Emlyn, wait! *Please* wait! *Wait*!' she cried, almost tripping on the trailing bag strap.

Emlyn stopped; he looked back, unsmiling, until Nia

caught up with him.

'I've got something for you,' she said, 'in my bag. And I want to tell you something about the dress you gave me!'

Emlyn began to stride out again.

Nia had to take little running steps in order to keep up with him. 'Hang on! Don't go so fast!' she exclaimed breathlessly.

'Are you coming back with me then?' he asked, slowing his pace a fraction.

'I'll come up to the chapel, but I'd better not come in!' She gulped for air. 'I had a bit of bother yesterday.'

'You're always having a bit of bother,' he remarked, but he slowed down sufficiently for her to heave her bag on to her shoulders. They were on the bridge now and the river obliterated all the town sounds.

'Emlyn,' she said. 'I think I saw your mam last night.'

'You what?' He stood quite still, trying to determine her expression, then he shook his head and resumed his frantic pacing.

When he had crossed the bridge, however, he did not continue up the hill to home but leapt down a steep bank, where nettles and brambles had been previously attacked to allow a narrow, safe passage to the river bank.

Nia followed, less adroitly, and found herself, with scratched hands and a dusty skirt, sitting beside Emlyn on the river bank. Before them the wide river snaked into the sunlight; behind and all about them, tall reeds concealed their presence from all but a moorhen, stepping daintily over shining stones.

They sat silently contemplating the water until Emlyn said, 'Go on, then!'

'Iolo had a spider in′ a matchbox.' Nia frowned, wondering if she had begun at the wrong place. 'The box

117

got wet down by the river; he gave it to me to look after.'
She ploughed on. 'It belonged to Gwyn Griffiths really.
You know about Gwyn Griffiths, don't you?'

'Huh!' was all Emlyn said.

'I mean, I know you know him,' Nia floundered. 'But
he's not like other boys, you know that, don't you?
Because of what happened in the churchyard.' She
glanced at Emlyn but he gave her no encouragement.

'Well, this spider, it was like silver and it sort of glowed.
I put the box down somewhere in my bedroom and then I
. . . well, I hope you don't mind, but I put on your mam's
dress. The one your dad gave me yesterday, like blossom.
It was your mam's, wasn't it?'

Emlyn nodded.

'The spider had made this cobweb, like a mirror it was –
shining.' Nia stared out at the water remembering the
glimmering shapes in the web. 'An' I could see my
reflection in it; only it wasn't me, it was your mother, I'm
sure it was. She had long dark hair, see, and big dark eyes
and . . .'

'Don't!' Emlyn jumped up and crashed his way through
the dense, dry reeds, then he swung round and came back
to her. He stood looking down at her, with his hands in his
pockets and said quietly, 'I didn't finish about the night
my mam went. I didn't tell you all of it.'

'I know,' Nia said, and waited.

Emlyn crouched beside her He spoke quietly and
unemotionally. 'She was wearing that dress, because it
was their wedding anniversary. It was all so good at the
beginning; they had wine and gave me some, and they
danced in the field, to some music on the old wind-up
gramophone. But then it all went wrong.' He gritted his
teeth, biting on a puzzle that still tormented him. 'There
118

was this wind, like I said, come up from nowhere. It made such a racket and the baby was crying and crying. It got dark and my mam was going on about the baby an' how we shouldn't be living in a place so small and cold and with no electricity. And my dad got mad; he shouted at her to "shut up" and she yelled back and pushed at one of the wooden animals, and somehow it must have knocked the heater over, because the next thing I saw, it was lying on its side and Mam was screaming with flames all round her, but Dad pulled the bedclothes off and wrapped her up in them, and put the fire out!'

'Was she burnt?'

Emlyn shrugged. 'Not much. Not badly. Dad saved her, see. But that wasn't the end of it. I went to sleep for a bit, and so did Dad I suppose, because when I woke up I saw him running into the field in his pyjamas. I got out of bed and followed him.' He took a deep breath which he expelled in a long sigh. His next words were spoken to the water, low and stiltingly. 'My mam was there right at the top of the bank, where the field goes down and down to the river. She'd got a big pile of my dad's paintings, heaped like a Guy Fawkes' bonfire, an' she'd poured paraffin on them, you could smell it, and she'd set them alight. She was throwing them into the river on a long branch, all flames: little bits were flying up into the sky. All Dad's work: all burning! And my mam was yelling she'd go mad if she stayed here. But we reckoned she was mad already.'

It all made sense now. The warnings. The fear and the suspicion in Pendewi. A fire and a mother driven mad. Flames in the air and in the river. 'Have you forgiven her?' Nia asked.

'Of course I have.' He hugged his knees and almost smiled, remembering, perhaps, a happier time, when his

119

mother had worn the dress in a sunny place, far away from
damp green Wales. 'She's waiting for me, maybe, in that
moon she went to, wondering why I haven't come to her.
Someone knows where she is, but they're not telling.'

Nia took Iolo's matchbox from her bag and opened it a
little. 'There's something special about this spider,' she
said. 'It belonged to Gwyn; but he's got Fly. You should
have this!' She put the box into Emlyn's hand.

He regarded the box. 'Can't take a spider for a walk!' he
remarked.

'No, but perhaps . . . perhaps you'll see your mam in a
web, like I did.'

He didn't reject her suggestion, but he stared at her very
hard and put the box in his pocket.

Nia got to her feet. 'I'd better go now,' she said. 'I
missed the cake yesterday.'

She scrambled up the bank, but Emlyn didn't follow
and, when she looked back from the bridge, nothing
moved beside the slowly misting river.

There was *bara brith* for tea, everyone's favourite; moist,
fruity and delicious. Two whole loaves were consumed
at a sitting.

Nia couldn't sleep afterwards. She took her canvas to
the bathroom and began to cut a mountain out of mottled
grey leather: her mother's gloves, once smart and best,
now torn and marked from holding baskets and babies'
hands. Something called her to the window, not a sound,
but a feeling, somehow, that something was taking place
outside that she should see.

The frosted glass distorted form and colour in the street.
Things changed but had no features. She slid the window
up a fraction, and knelt down to peer through the gap.
Nothing.

She pulled the window further, widening the gap enough to put her head out. Nothing in the street. But up on the bridge something moved, pale yellow in the deadening glare of the street lights, but probably white. Small creatures crossing the bridge: children, no bigger than herself, for the stones of the bridge wall came shoulder high.

Children out later than midnight! One, two, three, four, five! Nia counted them. Boys or girls? She couldn't tell. They were too far away, their heads concealed in hoods or scarves. Were they the 'things' Gwyn had talked of: the icy creatures who had taken his sister? They were on the hill now, walking to where a lamp still burned in the chapel window.

She slid the window down, careless of its rattle, rolled up her canvas and ran back to bed. She was trembling and for comfort clutched Iolo's blue monster which had fallen from his arms.

It was all wrong out there. Something terrible had happened. Something unstoppable. Should she run to Emlyn? No, they would stop her, take her. Nia folded herself over the soft woolly monster and screwed up her eyes. She found herself humming, low and monotonously, her head beneath the blankets, trying to blot out what she had seen, telling herself that there were no unearthly children moving towards the chapel.

When she fell asleep at last, it was to dream of herself, almost a baby, playing in the earth near the gate at Tŷ Llŷr. The soil was soft in her hands. She was poking little seeds into the ground, planting and playing. Someone was singing in the lane, and when she looked up she saw a woman with dark hair and a girl beside her, equally dark, holding white flowers, like stars.

122

The girl knelt beside Nia and laid the flowers on the ground. She took the seeds and planted them in a neat row under the sycamore, where the gate would not disturb them. Her dark hair brushed the earth. She was smiling as she worked, and she smelt of roses.

But you can't dream the smell of roses. Was it a memory?

Next morning a dusting of frost outlined the roofs and railings in Pendewi. The frost did not sparkle: there was no sun. Tiny beads of moisture hung in the air, motionless and cold. Damp penetrated the childrens' clothes: sleeves clung: shoes slipped. Beside the school gates, violet and yellow irises leaned forlornly, their petals turned to icy paper.

The climate in Pendewi had slipped.

The day had no shape. Within the school a cycle of learning and playing took place, while outside nothing changed. And when the children went home, afternoon seemed like cold, grey dawn.

Emlyn was not hurrying as he usually did. Nia had to wait for him to fall into step beside her. He seemed to have difficulty in finding his direction, though it only lay forward. He wandered from side to side, jostled by other children, uninterested and dreamy. The street was almost deserted by the time they reached Number 6.

'Did you . . . did you see anything last night?' Nia ventured, uncertain as to whether Emlyn was even aware of her.

He turned to look at her. The moist air made his face glossy. It looked like a face full of tears. He said nothing.

'The spider?' she gently reminded him. 'Did you see a

123

cobweb?'

He seemed to find speech an effort, but at last he said, 'Yes!'

'And did you see anything?' She dared not mention his mother's name. The climate seemed to forbid it.

He stared at her, thoughtfully, then shrugged.

'Tell me, please!'

He shook his head. 'No, I can't,' he said. He turned away but Nia caught at his sleeve.

'Please tell me,' she begged. 'Did you see your mam?'

He hesitated and then said, 'I saw her . . . but I still don't know where she is. There was more in the web. It made me want . . . I can't tell you what I saw!' He shook her off and drew away.

Rejected, Nia swung round and opened the black door, passed through it and slammed it behind her.

It could have been a stranger out there, not Emlyn who was always full of life and sometimes anger. Was it the children? What had he seen in the web, that was tugging at his mind? Would they lead him out of this world to see his mother?

Nia was too distracted to work on her collage that night, and the following day brought her no comfort. Emlyn was more remote than ever. As the days passed he seemed to fade. He was not eating, she could tell; he had become two sizes thinner than his clothes.

Taking a chance, one evening, Nia ran up to the chapel after tea. 'Just going to see Gwyneth,' she called to the voices scattered about Number 6, and didn't wait for an interrogation.

Idris Llewelyn was alone, applying giant splodges of yellow to a huge canvas. 'Emlyn's not here,' he informed Nia. 'Been off in the evenings lately. Thought he'd been with you.'

'No, he hasn't! I'm worried, Mr Llewelyn. Emlyn doesn't seem . . . right, if you know what I mean.'

'He doesn't, does he?' The painter sighed and scrubbed his brush on the sleeve of his black boiler suit.

'What d'you think's the matter, then?' She tried to get his attention by sidling round behind his canvas and tapping her foot.

He took up another brush. 'I wouldn't know, would I?'

'Well, you ought to!' Nia said. 'You ought to be worried. I am!'

'Look, girl!' He flung his brush on to a paint-spattered chair beside him. 'I am worried. I'm worried about this,' he jabbed a finger at his canvas. 'It's for an exhibition, see, and it's not ready!'

It hadn't occurred to Nia that adults had exhibitions, too. She shuffled away from him. Mr Llewelyn was obviously too preoccupied to notice the change in his son.

She left the chapel and returned to the town slowly, surveying hills and woods: watching for a boy who might be walking alone. But Emlyn Llewelyn was hidden with a mysterious someone or something who was slowly extinguishing him.

10
Orchard
of the
Moon

Only one person could help. She would have to make a confession, but in secret, somewhere where Gwyn Griffiths would listen and advise.

The cold mist shifted to the mountain. Next morning Gwyn's black hair glistened in the sun that had appeared to cheer the flowers in Pendewi.

'Is it cold up there, on the mountain?' Nia asked, surprising Gwyn and Alun as they talked together in the playground before school.

'It's cold!' Gwyn affirmed.

And I bet you know why, she thought. The boys were being conspiratorial again.

'I found something of yours,' she said. 'Iolo found it, really. A spider.'

Gwyn's reaction was more than she had hoped for. 'Where?' he demanded. 'Where is it?'

'At home, in a matchbox,' she lied. She had to get him to Number 6, somehow, in order to confide her problem.

'Come back with us, tonight,' Alun suggested. 'You can pick it up from there. Your dad'll fetch you after, won't he?'

'You've got it safe, then?' Gwyn asked.

'Oh yes!'

Emlyn Llewelyn passed just then. He looked in their direction. Gwyn returned his cousin's vacant stare: he seemed perturbed by Emlyn's appearance. Something passed between them, silently, an understanding that even Alun did not share.

Later, after school, Gwyn went home with the Lloyds.

Mrs Lloyd was not surprised, but quickly rang Gwyn's mother to ask if he should not stay for tea; she had barely enough sausages for her family.

Gwyn and Alun followed Nia to her room. Iolo was safely munching afternoon crisps in front of the television.

'Well, where is it then, and what has it been doing?'

Gwyn scanned the room, stepping over boxes and toys.

Nia shut the door and leant against it. She would have to hold Gwyn until she had wrung a promise from him. She did not know whether he would help his cousin.

'It's not here,' she said flatly.

Gwyn swung round.

'Aw, no!' Alun sank on to Nia's bed. 'What the heck are you up to, Nia?'

'I gave it to Emlyn Llewelyn!'

Understanding dawned in Gwyn. 'Why?' he asked.

'Because it's special, isn't it? Because it made a cobweb, there,' she pointed at the wardrobe, 'shiny-like, and I saw a woman in it, Emlyn's mother. I was wearing her dress, and . . .' Gwyn's expression was beginning to alarm her, 'so I gave the spider to Emlyn because you've got Fly and he's got nothing, and . . . and . . .' she clung to the door handle. Words were slipping out of her unevenly and too fast, but she couldn't check them. 'I thought he needed to see his mam but . . . it's all gone wrong, hasn't it? Something's swallowing him up, trying to take him . . .

127

there were children on the bridge after midnight, five of them going to the chapel, they were very pale and . . . '

'When?' Gwyn's dark eyes seemed to burn.

'Four days ago.'

'What? You stupid girl, why didn't you tell me?' Gwyn looked older than any boy she had known. She could feel another presence standing there. It made her limp. 'We must go there – stop them – if we're able!' Gwyn commanded.

'Where?' she cried. 'Who?'

'To the chapel!' He didn't answer her second question.

'They won't let her,' Alun said. 'They've forbidden it.'

'We'll see!' Gwyn took Nia by the shoulders and moved her out of his way. He opened the door. 'Get the dress!' he commanded, and was gone.

Alun, following his friend, looked back into the room and scolded, 'Why can't you do anything right?' He slammed the door behind him.

Muffled voices slipped between the sounds of Catrin's piano and a television presenter: Gwyn's voice and her father's, arguing.

Nia knelt beside her bed. She drew the pale blossomy dress into the light, then pulled the rolled canvas towards her. She laid it flat. Once she had thought it would be a masterpiece, but it was nothing, just a few scraps of coloured stuff, stitched and glued. It would never be finished.

She got to her feet and took her scissors from the drawer, then knelt again. 'Nia-can't-do-nothing,' she told the poppies that Nain Griffiths had dyed with such care. 'Nia is wicked, yes, and stupid. Nia's getting worse. Cut! Cut! Cut! Cutting Miss Oliver's lace, cutting socks! Cut your work, Nia Lloyd! It's back to the nursery class with you!

128

You'll never finish! Never!'

The small, sharp scissors glinted. She began to cut where she had started; where grey smoke drifted from a chimney. Cut! Cut! Cut!

'Don't!' Gwyn Griffiths was there, glaring at her from the door. 'Stupid girl! Don't!'

Nia was bewildered. She sat back. Her scissors dropped on to the canvas. 'How did you know?'

'I know! I'm nosy, see! I like to know things. Leave it: it's a masterpiece. Roll it up, quick!' Gwyn was a boy again, almost. 'Emlyn needs us. Cutting won't help, will it? Will it?' His voice changed with the questions, became that older, wiser voice, full of authority.

'No!' Stunned, Nia rolled up her canvas.

'Hurry!'

'Where are we going?'

'To the chapel.'

'Do they know: Mam and Dad?'

'They know. I've fixed it. Come on, and bring the dress!'

Was he all-powerful? Nia pushed her canvas into the secret darkness beneath her bed, picked up the dress and followed Gwyn.

Down the stairs, across the hall, through the front door, making no effort to tread lightly. The piano shrilled, the television blared, and Mr and Mrs Lloyd sat in the kitchen, bemused. That Gwyn Griffiths! He had a way of making you do things – Good God, what were children coming to?

Gwyn closed the black door against the Lloyd's mixed-bag of noises. 'It's OK,' he said. 'Don't look so downcast. And hurry!' He began to run and Nia pursued him, past Miss Oliver's grey house where unlucky lace curtains

129

concealed someone murdering Mendelssohn; past the other chapel where Mary McGoohan was accompanying herself on the organ; past Police Constable Jones, who was humming in the street. The town was in good voice today, while Nia's throat was tight with apprehension.

How could Gwyn run up a hill so steep? They were out of the town now with all the singing sounds behind them. Nia stopped, gasping for air.

'Come on!' Gwyn commanded and she ran again, clutching the blossom dress, too breathless to wonder what the boy-magician wanted. He was on the chapel steps; she could hear him banging on the blue and gold door and then he vanished through it.

Nia reached the chapel, expecting to hear Idris Llewelyn shouting at his nephew. But there were no sounds. She peered inside. Gwyn was standing beside a wooden beast with a fiery orange mane, a unicorn with vacant yellow eyes. 'I had forgotten,' he said. 'I came here, once, when we were friends.' He seemed to have lost, momentarily, the resolve which had brought him to the place.

'Gwyn, what shall we do?' she asked.

'Arianwen's here,' he said.

'Arianwen?' Nia saw no one.

'Come in and close the door!'

'But . . .'

'Do it!'

Nia obeyed. She went over to Gwyn who was holding something. She saw the snow spider glowing in the palm of his hand. 'I call her Arianwen,' he said, 'white-silver. She came in the snow, from another world. My sister sent her.'

'I don't understand,' Nia said.

'But you will believe me, won't you, if I try to tell you?'

130

'I'll believe!'

He sat on the painter's chair, while she nervously paced round the wooden animals, listening for approaching footsteps, but hearing only Gwyn.

'Two years ago, nearly, just after my ninth birthday, I threw an old brooch into the wind. Nain told me to. It was a very ancient brooch, twisted and patterned, silver and bronze; it came from Nain's great-great-grandmother. They say she was a witch. I threw it from the mountain where Bethan disappeared. Snow fell afterwards and in the snow on my shoulder I found Arianwen.'

Nia gazed at the tiny creature that had lived in her room for a while.

'She came from that other planet,' Gwyn went on, 'and in her webs she showed me the place where my sister lives now. And I saw the pale children who took her away.'

'On the bridge!' Nia cried. 'They're here, aren't they?'

Gwyn didn't answer her. 'There's something I never told anyone,' he said. 'Bethan tried to take me back with her and part of me wanted to go, but I belong here, I feel like I've got roots going very deep, down into the time when there were magicians where we live now.'

'Emlyn hasn't,' Nia said. 'Emlyn hasn't got anything. He'll want to go.'

'So we must find his mother and then he'll have something, won't he?'

Nia nodded, knowing that Gwyn was going to ask something of her. 'Your auntie, Elinor, she isn't out there, is she?'

'No, she's still here and my dad knows where, but I can't ask him. He thinks he's saved her, see. He doesn't know Emlyn like we do.'

'So, what must I do?'

132

'Put on the dress!'

'Over my clothes?'

'Over your clothes. Don't be afraid.'

'What if someone comes?'

'Do it!' he said solemnly. 'Arianwen shows us what she thinks we should see, whether it's hours or years or miles away. Time and distance, they're all the same to her.'

Nia slipped the dress over her head. Nothing could interfere with what she and Gwyn were about to do. She felt the cool silky stuff sliding against her skin. If there was a place for spells then it was surely here. The beasts and butterflies, the long windows and the many-coloured paintings began to drift out of her vision; a boy with brown hair looked down, smiling, from beside a river, and then he was gone behind a shining, widening screen of gossamer. Gwyn's spider was spinning; climbing and falling, weaving and swinging across the wall beside Emlyn's bed.

'Hold tight! Stay very still! Don't run, even if there's pain!' Distance or time had come between her and the voice but the words, though faint, held her fast. She could see the dress now, in the web that was a mirror; she could see the face that wasn't hers, and the dark hair. She felt unaccountably sad. Beside her a baby cried, on and on, above the clamour of the wind. She was angry now and shouting, pushing out at the thing that had made her angry.

'What am I doing? Where am I going? Who am I? Gwyn?' She called, and again, 'Gwyn, where are you?'

And the old, wise voice replied, 'Stay, Nia! Don't run!'

Flames crept into the web; guttering gold streaks flared into silver; dazzling scarlet fingers caught at the dress and leapt up at her face.

'Help me!' she screamed. 'I hate you!' she shouted to someone she couldn't see.

'Don't move, Nia!'

But she couldn't help herself. While small, frightened Nia clung to the space in which she existed, her reflection fled through dark fields carrying a baby. She ran along familiar paths, down into a valley where moonlight made strange shapes and shadows, towards small, ancient trees that bent under a canopy of blossom; an orchard planted in a crescent – like the moon!

'Where are you going, Nia?'

'I'm going to the moon,' she cried. 'Of course, the moon! The orchard of the moon! That's where she is – Perllan yr hanner Lleuad; those were her words, but Emlyn only heard her say 'half-moon'. Elinor Llewelyn is in the valley where the cold flowers grow!'

'Come out then, Nia! Step back, towards my voice!'

But Nia couldn't move. She was caught in the web. A silly fly bound by strands of the past and another person's life. The spell was too powerful, she couldn't break out.

'Nia! Nia!' The voice was nearer, its power increasing.

Nia held her breath, leant backwards and took one laboured step away from the mirror. As she did so, the glittering glass rippled like the sea and tore apart. Branches of blossom drifted up through the sky of butterflies, fragmenting into tiny flakes that melted to nothing.

She felt a hand on her shoulder; someone tapping gently.

When she turned she saw a face as old and as tired as she felt. Gwyn looked utterly exhausted.

'It's as though we've been asleep,' she said.

'Not me. I've never worked so hard,' he replied. 'And

we can't rest now. There's more to do.'

'Yes,' she said meekly.

She stepped out of the dress and laid it on Emlyn's bed while Gwyn took his spider from the bedpost, where it had come to rest.

'We must go to my aunt now,' he said, 'and make her come back to her family before it's too late.'

Gwyn opened the chapel door and almost walked into Idris Llewelyn who stood there, angry at finding strangers in his home, astonished to see who they were. 'Beth wyt 'in eiseau, Gwyn Griffiths?' he asked coldly. 'What do you want?'

11

Soldiers at Dusk

'We are looking for your wife,' Gwyn said.

'You won't find her here!' Idris Llewelyn took a step towards Gwyn. His fists were clenched.

Gwyn stood his ground. 'I know, and it's wrong,' he said. 'She should be here and she will.'

'And who are you, boy, to think that you can reconcile people who were torn apart by your own family?'

Nia saw arrogance flare up in Gwyn but he resisted the temptation to tell who and what he really was. 'I'm going to do what you should have done, long ago, for Emlyn,' he said. 'You never bothered even to search for your wife, so proud you are, Idris Llewelyn!'

To Nia's horror, the painter laughed. It was not a happy sound. On his face Nia saw a loss that was too unbearable to speak of. She plucked at Gwyn's arm, hoping to stem any more unpleasant truths that he might fling out. But Gwyn had not finished.

'You're going to lose Emlyn, too,' he said. 'Where is he now?'

Idris Llewelyn wasn't laughing when he answered. 'He's been gone all night!' And turning to Nia, he said, 'I'm worried, girl, like you. Find him for me, will you?

You're the . . . '

He could not say what he intended, for they were interrupted by the screech of brakes. Gwyn's father glared out from his Landrover. He could see the children standing inside the open door, beyond Idris Llewelyn. 'What're you doing there, boy?' he shouted.

Idris swung round. The two men looked at each other, but said nothing.

Gwyn ran past his uncle and Nia followed. They climbed into the back of the Landrover while the engine was still throbbing, but as they drove off Nia called to the lonely man on the chapel steps, 'I'll find him, Mr Llewelyn. I promise I will!'

Gwyn's father accelerated away from the chapel. The Landrover roared up the hill. He committed a crime here, Nia thought: kidnapping, of a sort, and he doesn't like visiting the scene of his crime.

Mr Griffiths was not in a mood for questions it seemed. He drove fast and remained silent. When they reached Tŷ Bryn, however, and the children climbed out, he suddenly asked, 'What's Nia Lloyd doing here, then?'

'She's come for tea,' Gwyn airily replied. 'We're going up the mountain first to look for something.'

Did his father guess? If so, he gave no sign. 'What were you doing in that – place?' He couldn't bring himself to say the name.

'They're relations,' Gwyn retorted. 'Everyone needs relations!'

He took Nia's hand and led her back on to the lane that wound and narrowed between thick hedges until it became a sheep track in an open field.

'I'm going to run now,' Gwyn warned her. 'Can you keep it up?'

Nia nodded. His urgency inspired her. 'I'll probably race you,' she said.

They took off and ran side by side, away from the track and across the steep field where their feet twisted into unaccustomed angles on the hard, listing land.

Gwyn drew ahead and reached the valley before her. He waited until she was beside him again and they looked down into Half Moon Orchard. Frost had snapped at the blossoms and petals were drifting from the bare branches on to the white flowers beneath.

'They're so bright,' Nia said. 'You could see them from miles in the air.'

'Even further,' muttered Gwyn. '*They* have seen them.'

They began to walk down into the valley, through the oak wood and through the flowers that had grown knee-high, turning the atmosphere above them into arctic air.

And there was the stone cottage, with a light in the window and wood smoke curving from the chimney.

Gwyn marched up to the door and knocked. Elinor Llewelyn opened it: she stared at Gwyn for a moment, then smiled, relieved to recognise her visitor. 'Gwyn!' she said. 'Your father told you, then?'

'My father told me nothing,' Gwyn answered. 'Can we come in?'

The woman hesitated. She had not seen Nia at first. 'Who is this?' She had become nervous, her hand plucking at a string of beads round her neck.

'It's Nia Lloyd from Tŷ Llŷr. You remember!'

Elinor Llewelyn relaxed. 'I thought it might be . . . '

'Bethan?' Gwyn said. 'No. She's gone!'

'Of course!' His aunt stood back while they passed her into a dark room that was sparsely furnished, clean and tidy: a fire burned in a small black grate. The floorboards were polished, the rug thin and frayed. A boy of two or three played on a bench beside the window.

'This is Geraint,' she said, and the boy ran and hid his face in her skirt. 'He doesn't see many people,' she explained. 'Will you sit down? I've got orange juice, I think, and . . . and biscuits.'

Her voice was ordinary, light and pleasant, and her face was not as beautiful as the reflection Nia had come to know. This woman looked older, her hair greyer, her eyes deeper and ringed with blue shadows.

'If it wasn't for your father, I wouldn't see a soul,' she went on. 'I don't go out much, see. I can't since . . . '

'It must be lonely,' Nia said, looking at Emlyn's little brother.

'Well . . . I suppose . . . but . . . ' again the woman seemed unable to form a sentence. She backed away to a tall green cupboard where she found mugs and orange juice, and a tin of biscuits.

The children took her offerings and sat side by side on the bench amongst Geraint's toys.

'I think you'll have to come out soon, Auntie Elinor,' Gwyn said.

'Come out?' She didn't sit with them but paced nervously beside the fire while little Geraint still clung to her.

'For Emlyn's sake,' Gwyn said. 'Your other son. He needs to see you. Something is happening to him. They will take him away.'

'Take him? But his father is good to him? Ivor, your father, tells me what I need to know. He tells me they're well, my husband and my son. And . . . and I could never go back to them, now . . . I don't like going out.'

'Are you ill, Auntie Elinor?' Gwyn asked, carefully.

'Ill? Yes!' she replied. 'Since the fire, you see. I feel safe here. Your father brings me all I want. And your mam, Glenys, she brings my pills and clothes and toys for Geraint, little things you didn't need, Gwyn.'

Nia suddenly remembered the knitted woollen soldier she had found at Tŷ Llŷr.

'Mam said she'd taken them to Oxfam,' Gwyn said, almost to himself.

'Oh we do go out, you know,' Elinor went on, 'early when no one's about, don't we, Geraint? Sometimes we walk to the top of the track. Ivor picks us up in the Landrover. But we never go to Pendewi. I could never go there again, never. They know what's best for me, don't they?' She began to bite her nails and Nia was reminded of Alun who used to do that when he was angry and only eight years old. He'd grown out of the habit long ago.

The children stared at Elinor Llewelyn in dismay. She appeared to have an illness that couldn't be named. Could such a frightened and sick person help anyone?

'Who planted those flowers?' Gwyn asked, hoping to jolt his aunt away from memories that distressed her.

'Oh those? A girl.' Elinor brightened visibly. 'Such a lovely girl, like Bethan, only fair. She stumbled in here one winter time, when Geraint was a baby. It was quite wonderful. There'd been a heavy fall of snow and we hadn't seen a soul for weeks but there she was, smiling in at the window. I brought her in, of course, but she didn't seem to feel the cold. Such a funny child; we talked about flowers, I don't know why, and trees, the things that I shared with Bethan.' She was calm now, recalling happier times. 'Before the girl left,' she went on, 'she gave me some seeds. ''Plant them under the trees when the snow has gone,'' she said, ''and next year you will have flowers

141

in your orchard, flowers like stars, and then we can always find you.'' '

Nia felt Gwyn tense beside her. He put his hand on hers, whether to alert her or comfort himself she couldn't tell, but his taut fingers pressed so hard she almost cried out.

'What was her name?' he asked.

'Eirlys!' His aunt was smiling now. 'I remember because it's the Welsh for snowdrop and she came in the snow.'

Gwyn jumped up, pulling Nia with him. 'We have to go now,' he told his aunt, 'and if Emlyn comes here, tell him to wait for us!'

'Emlyn? Oh no! He won't. You mustn't tell him!' The woman instantly became anxious again.

'Don't you want to see him?' Nia asked accusingly.

'I do! do! I wanted to go back for him so many times. But he knew where I was and he never came. Besides Idris would have made me stay and I couldn't. You're only children. You don't understand what it's like, wanting something but being afraid. The pills help me to forget, and it's best like that.'

Nia began to wish she had never found Elinor Llewelyn. But she had reason to thank her. She pulled the knitted woollen soldier out of her pocket. 'Geraint must have dropped this in my garden,' she said, 'when you went to look after my poppies.'

Elinor took the soldier. 'So he did!' She smiled. 'Thank you, Nia. There was no one there, so I took it on myself to do a bit of gardening. It was sad to see lovely Tŷ Llŷr so empty and alone.'

Gwyn was already hovering impatiently outside the door. Nia joined him and they began to run, calling 'Goodbye' to Elinor Llewelyn, though she had already closed the door.

They ran through the cold flowers and up the path, and this time Nia did not panic, because Gwyn knew the way. He had been there before, when the cottage was deserted, but never since his aunt had lived there. 'Dad told me it wasn't safe,' Gwyn said. 'I didn't think to ask why. I just never bothered to come and look.'

When Nia climbed out of the valley, Gwyn had increased the distance between them. He was leaping ahead like a wild animal, but when the farmhouse was in sight he stopped and waited for her.

Nia caught up with him and as they walked down the track together she asked, 'Is your aunt mad then, Gwyn? To run away from her own family, to want to forget them?'

He shook his head. 'It was the baby,' he said. 'Mam told me that mothers do strange things when they are frightened and have a baby. It's protection, like animals and birds. Even our old hens go mad if you touch their chicks.'

'They don't stay mad,' Nia remarked, 'when the chicks are grown.'

'No. Then it's something I can't explain. My dad went mad when Bethan disappeared. Perhaps that's why he took special care of Auntie Elinor: he understood. He didn't get better until . . . ' Gwyn began to run again.

'Until what?' Nia tried to keep up though her legs and her ribs were aching.

'Until she came back. Until Eirlys came. I'm scared, Nia,' he confessed, 'about the flowers she planted.'

'She?' Nia was confused.

'Don't you understand? Bethan was Eirlys!'

She stood quite still. Pieces of a jigsaw began to move

143

closer It was like glimpsing a picture through spaces in a cloud. 'Bethan?' she breathed.

Gwyn stopped too. He looked at her. 'She must have had seeds with her, in her pocket, when they took her to that other place, and when she came back she brought the seeds with her, only they had changed, like she had. Things that grow in the dark, they're pale. Bethan meant no harm; she only wanted to find her way back to Perllan yr hanner Lleuad. But *they'll* see them, the others, it's like a landmark, shouting at them, and they'll go there, where it's safe and quiet, and they'll wait and take someone, a child, they only take children.'

'But they're here already!'

'Only five, you said. There'll be more, many more.'

'We must tell someone. Get help.'

'You can't explain things like this,' Gwyn said. 'I know; I've tried. It's too hard for people to understand.'

'What must we do?'

'There were three of us once,' he muttered. 'We're stronger together.' He was looking into a space above her head, and then, becoming aware of her scrutiny, he said, 'Wait, and think!'

They went into the farmhouse and Mrs Griffiths, so happy to see Nia again, did not ask why she was there, but spread the table with hard-boiled eggs and salad and a newly-baked malt loaf and chocolate cake. Nia did her best to do justice to such treats, but her stomach refused to accept more than a few mouthfuls.

'What is it, cariad? Are you going down with something? How are they at home?' Mrs Griffiths asked, concerned for her favourite visitor.

'Gareth's OK. His leg gets in the way, though,' Nia said. 'And Mam's that tired. I expect it's the sponge I had for dinner. I'll feel better soon. Can I take some cake home with me?' She was glad Nerys was not there, to glare at her for asking such a question.

'Of course! You might have to wait a bit, though. Gwyn's dad wants to do some fencing on the lane before dark, those Tŷ Llŷr lambs keep getting out.'

'Dad never did his fences proper,' Nia said, and then, because she'd been disloyal, added, 'He's good at butchering, though. He's great at that; people come for miles!'

'That's nice, isn't it?' Mrs Griffiths smiled uncertainly.

The children helped to clear the table and then went to see Gwyn's white rabbits in the orchard. They were in separate hutches now. Gwyn lifted a hinged door above the female's sleeping quarters and Nia, crouched beside him, saw a bed of soft fur. 'It's where the babies will be born,' he told her, 'but we don't dare look for a while, or she'll eat them. They go peculiar-like when they give birth.'

'Like your Auntie Elinor,' Nia said.

'A bit like that.'

It was much darker than usual for an early summer evening; and cold. The rabbits wouldn't eat their supper of favourite weeds. They sat rigid on their hind legs, alert and anxious. The birds had fallen silent and even the chorus of ever-hungry lambs had died to an intermittent plaintive bleat.

Something rippled through the air, not a breeze, but more like a shock wave: a sound like silent screaming.

Gwyn stood up. 'Aw heck!' he said quietly. 'Aw heck, Nia. It's happening.' He clutched his thick hair with both hands.

'What?' she asked, frightened by his attitude.

145

'The children are here, and I didn't call. I didn't make the ship; the seaweed is safe in my drawer. They've come for someone, like they came for Bethan. Can't you feel it?'

Nia didn't need to answer. Cold and dread had caused her to wrap her arms tight about herself.

They stood staring helplessly at each other and then a movement by the gate broke the tension and Nain Griffiths came towards them, tall under the apple trees, and dressed in forest green.

'I heard children in the lane,' she said, 'and I thought it was you.'

'We're here,' Gwyn said. 'We've been here all the time.'

'I saw a boy,' Nain went on, 'and he was alone. But there were others in the woods beside him. I heard them laughing.'

'Emlyn knows,' Nia whispered. 'He knows where his mam is. They're taking him there.'

'And the others will be waiting!' Gwyn's voice cracked and then he was seizing Nia's hand, dragging her through the orchard, up the path and through the gate. 'Tell them we've gone to look for someone,' he shouted to his grandmother as they pounded towards the field.

Their race, this time, was desperate. Nia felt as though the earth was rocking upside down. They ran on dark rolling clouds in an icy stream of air. The only warmth in the whole world was caught between her hand and Gwyn's, and then he let go of her and, as he drew ahead, she lost him in a mist of freezing vapour.

Her feet and instinct took her to the place, and on the woodland path she caught up with Gwyn as he stood waiting for her. He was watching Emlyn Llewelyn walking toward the Orchard of the Half Moon, and the cottage

146

where his mother was.

Emlyn would soon be with his mam. Nia sighed with relief. She let herself sink on to the path and sat there, relaxed and almost happy. Gwyn took several paces away from her. Something about the set of his shoulders, the way he moved, would not let her rest. When she stood again she was petrified by the prospect before her.

There were children crowding into the cottage garden: pale, graceful children; hundreds: they moved in from the trees like streams of thistledown, murmuring softly, their voices gentle as rain.

'They are ancient,' Gwyn said. 'But only in wisdom. Their bones are not brittle. They will not die – unless they are afraid. I know this!'

Nia knew that Emlyn had forgotten his mother. He could only see the children, so beautiful, almost translucent in the dusk.

'They'll take him, Gwyn,' she wanted to cry, but even had she been capable, Gwyn wouldn't have heard her: he had gone and something else was where he should have been: a frosty tree stump: a man kneeling under a cloak that reflected all the bright shades in the sky, and hair silver with sunlight.

There were words in the air, rising and falling like insistent, monotonous music. Names perhaps: Math, Lord of Gwynedd, Gwydion and Gilfaethwy. Names in the air, sung like a sacrament.

And once again, as in the churchyard, time held back and nothing moved, except the flowers, and they were growing. And Nia saw, or maybe dreamt, that from the flowers two men came: soldiers or princes, the way they used to be, with gold at their throats, and round their naked arms; with broad shining swords and patterned shields that gleamed like fire.

They dipped their swords, once, twice, as in a rite, together, and where fiery bronze touched the earth, flames came leaping round them.

If nothing else was real, the fire was. Nia could feel the heat on her face. But Emlyn wasn't moving. Fear or the children seemed to paralyse him and he would soon be engulfed by flames.

'Help him, Nia!' It was Gwyn's voice. He was beside her, tugging her hand. 'He's remembering.'

Nia couldn't move.

'I can't do it alone, Nia!'

The fire was white hot.

'It's an illusion, Nia. It won't hurt you. But I can't keep it!'

'No!' she shrank back.

'We must hold him, or he will go. I am losing myself . . .'

'I can't do nothing,' she moaned.

'We're in this together, Nia Lloyd!' the voice hissed in her ear, so close that she felt it in her head; she sprang away from it and ran with one boy, down towards the other who now seemed less substantial than the flames.

But she grasped one hand in both of hers, while Gwyn took the other, and they held and pulled him.

The fire spat and stank. It licked their feet and clothes like a hungry beast. And Emlyn was rooted in the ground, heavy as oak.

They pulled him until Nia thought that if her body didn't burn it would surely break, and then, slowly, he came with them.

Beyond the tall soldiers, Nia could see the children, pressing together, terrified by something that should not exist either in their world, or in the place they had invaded. They turned and screamed through the trees.

A mist of swimming white shapes escaped out on to the mountain and gathered into a cloud of snow: it seemed to shake the earth as it rose into the sky.

Before she fell, Nia thought she saw a billowing sail and a silver prow with dancing creatures on it passing overhead.

12
A
Masterpiece

They were all in the kitchen at Tŷ Bryn. Nia hardly remembered how they had come there.

It had been dark in Perllan yr Hanner Lleuad, and there had been a wind. They had gone to find Emlyn, she and Gwyn, but the world had rocked and they had fallen, all three, down together to the place where Emlyn's mother lived.

An earth tremor, Gwyn's father called it.

But the bruises on Nia's hands were red, like burns. Her father was there, without his butcher's apron, and he was stroking her head like he used to do, when she was a very little girl.

She couldn't see Gwyn.

Emlyn was there, on the big settle beside his own mother, who held him like she never wanted to let him go, and Geraint was sitting on Idris Llewelyn's knee.

But Nia couldn't see Gwyn.

Gwyn's father was there, grim by the stove. He had known where the children would be when Idris Llewelyn came banging on his door, and summer lightning shattered the sky.

Gwyn wasn't there.

Mrs Griffiths was pouring tea by the kitchen table. It was she who had carried Nia out of the valley. She had gone with her husband and Idris Llewelyn, under a sky as green as a field of spells. And they had found the children, dazed and bruised, with Elinor Llewelyn crying beside them. The wind had torn her roof away.

'Where is Gwyn?' Nia cried.

They all looked at her and Gwyn's mother said gently, 'He's resting, cariad.'

'Let me see him!'

'He's asleep!'

She didn't believe them. 'I want to see him!' she demanded.

So Mrs Griffiths took Nia into the front room and she saw Gwyn lying in a big armchair with a blanket over him. His eyes were closed and his face, beneath the cloud of black hair, looked like paper.

'The doctor's coming soon,' Mrs Griffiths told her. 'He'll put Gwyn right; he must!'

It seemed then that, not only Nia's voice, but her whole body yelled, 'He's not asleep!' And tears spilled out in a wave that left her breathless. She wiped them away again and again; as though they had no business there, when there were so many things to consider.

Mr Griffiths gripped her shoulders. 'He's not gone, girl,' he said. 'We'll get him right. Come away, now.'

As he drew her into the passage, the front door opened and Nain Griffiths stood there, in a cloak that shone darkly, like crow feathers.

'Give me my boy!' she said.

Without a word, Mr Griffiths went and lifted his son out of the chair. He put Gwyn, wrapped in the blanket, into Nain's arms, and although he was ten years old, his grandmother carried him into the night, as if he was nothing but a shadow.

Summer came swiftly after the storm: a scorching summer of cloudless skies and hours of sunshine that stretched from early dawn till long after bedtime.

Morgan-the-Smithy and his three sons worked shirtless out of doors. Nia watched them in the evenings, splashing themselves cool in the river, singing and swearing cheerfully at each other.

Six weeks went by and in those weeks so many things happened it was as if a train had thundered through the valley, throwing out goodwill like birthday parcels.

Idris Llewelyn sold his yellow-patterned painting to a gallery in London; they wanted more if he could do them. They took his photo for the papers, with his wife and his two sons. How proud he was in his black boiler suit, holding a cheque for a thousand pounds.

Emlyn came back to school, quite his old self again, only now he was, 'that Emlyn whose dad sells paintings', and children queued up to talk to him.

Elinor Llewelyn left the cottage in Half Moon Orchard; she couldn't stay for her roof had fallen in. She and Geraint went to live in the Griffiths' farmhouse. She saw Emlyn and her husband every day, but nothing would persuade her to move back to the chapel. This unsatisfactory situation might have continued, had not help arrived from quite an unexpected quarter.

One afternoon Mr Lloyd came out of his shop, hot and a little irritable. It wasn't easy trying to sell meat from the window and keep it cool. His impatient family waited for their tea while he scrupulously scrubbed his hands in the sink, and then he said, in an off-hand way, 'Would Idris
152

Llewelyn think of living in Tŷ Llŷr? His wife would go there, I'm sure. There'd be no money involved – well not much – no one else wants it, and it'll fall down if it's empty longer. He can keep his chapel, just for work.'

Nia ran and hugged him, bloody apron and all.

'Hold on, girl,' he laughed. 'They haven't agreed. And it'll need a fair bit of work doing on it.'

Of course they did agree. Elinor had always loved Tŷ Llŷr, and Idris could turn his hand to any sort of building.

He and Ivor Griffiths, reconciled at last, spent a night in The Red Dragon inn, with Iestyn Lloyd, to seal the buying of Tŷ Llŷr. It was a night the town never forgot. They called it Llewelyn's night, for he was like a returning prince, now that he had a house and a wife, two fine sons and money in the bank. Pendewi Male Voice Choir was there, and you could hear the singing all the way to the sea.

But Nia remembered it because it was the night she finished her picture. She took the tiny pieces she had cut from the hem of Elinor Llewelyn's dress and sewed them in a half-circle on the side of the mountain, and beneath them she glued clusters of silver glitter, so that they appeared to reflect the stars in her midnight sky.

It was finished – yet incomplete.

She could have asked Emlyn's advice: he was an acceptable visitor now, and she could have taken it to Idris Llewelyn in his chapel studio, to ask what was missing. But she waited until Gwyn Griffiths had recovered.

He came to visit them a week after Llewelyn's night. He was still pale, but his grandmother's herbs had brought him to life. If it was shock that he had suffered from, as his father said it was, then why did his eyes look so weary and why did he stumble on the stairs? Nia knew that it was exhaustion, that he'd put too much of himself into the spell

153

that had brought ghosts back to Wales, to save his cousin.

After tea, when the other boys were playing in the river, Nia took Gwyn indoors to see her work.

She laid it out on the floor of her room and sat back, watching him.

Gwyn knelt beside the canvas. He observed it solemnly, while Nia waited anxiously.

'It's beautiful, Nia!' he said at last. 'It's a masterpiece. It's magic . . . '

'But,' she said anxiously, 'something's missing, isn't it?'

Gwyn frowned. 'No. Not really, it's only . . . there's no one there: no people: only birds and sheep.'

'Oh!' She gazed at the canvas for a moment. 'People change,' she said. 'They go and they die!'

Gwyn looked at her. 'In a way,' he said. Then he left her and went to join Alun by the river.

When he had gone she cut the shape of a girl out of her mother's shell-grey tights, and put it where the starry flowers grew in Perllan yr Hanner Lleuad. And in the oak wood she put a starling's feather: it could have been a holly tree or a shining cloak. Beyond the feather she glued strips of brown silk sprinkled with gold glitter, and in the centre of each strip, a silver circle, like the shield of a soldier, a prince – or a magician!

Her landscape was complete.

The following day the children in Standard Three had to submit their Project work.

They were all in the Assembly Hall, Miss Powell and the older children from Standard Four as well, brought in to help Mr James with his judging. The long table at the end of the hall was filling with papers, books and models. Gwyneth Bowen's story was three exercise books long, and her illustrations drew sighs of envy and admiration.

Then it was Nia's turn. She handed Mr James her long roll of canvas and he looked at her apprehensively before unrolling it. For a second Nia panicked. It was the wrong way up. They wouldn't understand. Then Miss Powell caught the other end and they held it up, two metres of it, high enough for everyone to see.

It went dead quiet and Nia's nose began to itch, though it hadn't done so for nearly a month, and she felt Gwyneth Bowen glaring at her.

There was sunlight in the hall. The stars, streams and flowers glittered. Nia had never seen her picture from a distance. She could hardly believe it was she who had put those brilliant colours and shapes together.

'Nia Lloyd, did anyone help you with this?' Mr James asked, astonished and disbelieving.

'No, sir!' Nia tried to say, but her throat had gone dry and the words came out as a guilty sort of cough.

Then, from the back of the room, Emlyn Llewelyn shouted, 'Nia did it herself, sir. I know. You can ask my dad. And don't you ever say she didn't!'

Everyone looked at him and then at Nia who felt very hot, and Mr James was too taken aback to make an issue of the impudence. 'Well!' he said, and, 'By heck, this is a helluva . . . '

He didn't realize he was swearing until everyone began to laugh and he felt Miss Powell staring at him.

'I think this is it, children, don't you?' he said, remembering his dignity. 'A masterpiece! We'll hang it right in the middle! Pride of place! Llongyfarchiadau, Nia Lloyd! Congratulations! By heck, this is something for the papers!'

Then everyone was clapping and stamping and

shouting, 'Hooray!' and banging Nia on the back. And when she left the Assembly Hall she knew she would never be Nia-can't-do-nothing again.

She went up to Llewelyn's chapel that evening. It was the last night that it would be a home and although the painter would come to work there, it would never be quite the same again.

The Griffiths family were there. The boys were kicking a ball round the field, little Geraint following Emlyn and screaming with delight. The parents watched and murmured to each other.

Nia stepped up on to the railings and looked over. She couldn't go in. They were all together now, one family, but not hers. She clung to the railings and watched them for a long time. They never saw her. She had brought them together, just as she'd always intended.

She stepped down into the road and became aware that someone was shouting her name.

Alun was running up the hill. 'It's come, Nia! The baby! Mam wants you!' he called.

Nia flew down towards him but Emlyn must have seen her. He came out on to the road and shouted, 'Nia! You'll come to Tŷ Llŷr, won't you? There's going to be loads of plums and the flowers are yours, they always will be!'

But she was too breathless to reply or turn to him. There were so many thoughts racing through her mind, above all the sudden realization that she wasn't in the middle any more.

If she was a little apprehensive ascending the last flight of stairs, she forgot everything when she found her family, crushed into the few spaces round the huge bed.

The boys were sitting on it, her sisters leaning on one side, and Mr Lloyd on the other.

Mrs Bennett, the midwife, was in the only chair. The baby had come that quick she was still breathless from bicycling two miles and running up three flights of stairs, and she overweight and old enough to retire.

'Come and see your sister, Nia,' Mrs Lloyd said. 'Beautiful, she is! And so like you!'

'Give her a name, girl!' Mr Lloyd drew her closer to the bed, where the baby lay in her mother's arms.

'It's your turn, Nia, to name the baby!' Catrin reminded her.

Nia approached, self-conscious and diffident. The baby looked solemnly out of her knitted white cocoon: her eyes were round and dark as berries. There was only one name for a baby like that.

'Let's call her Bethan!' Nia said.

JENNY NIMMO

The Snow Spider

'Time to find out if you are a magician!' said Gwyn's grandmother, as she gave him five strange birthday gifts. What could they mean? The piece of seaweed, the yellow scarf, the tin whistle, the twisted metal brooch and the small broken horse? Gwyn gave the brooch to the wind and, in return, there came a tiny silver spider, Arianwen. The snow spider . . .

So begins an extraordinary account of battles against evil and encounters with other worlds of snow and silver.

The first book in THE SNOW SPIDER trilogy.

The Chestnut Soldier

For three years Gwyn has not grown, and his magic powers have become a burden to him. Then Evan Llyr, a soldier seeks refuge in the village, and Gwyn has new conflicts to resolve. Gwyn feels a strange affinity with the soldier, but as autumn burns into the mountain, he knows he must do battle with him – a battle in which one of them will perish.

The Chestnut Soldier triumphantly concludes the trilogy begun with **The Snow Spider** and continued by **Emlyn's Moon.** It is an astonishing, beautiful story of the triumph of love and loyalty over hatred and evil.

A Selected List of Fiction from Mammoth

While every effort is made to keep prices low, it is sometimes necessary to increase prices at short notice. Mammoth Books reserves the right to show new retail prices on covers which may differ from those previously advertised in the text or elsewhere.

The prices shown below were correct at the time of going to press.

☐	416 13972 8	**Why the Whales Came**	Michael Morpurgo	£2.50
☐	7497 0034 3	**My Friend Walter**	Michael Morpurgo	£2.50
☐	7497 0035 1	**The Animals of Farthing Wood**	Colin Dann	£2.99
☐	7497 0136 6	**I Am David**	Anne Holm	£2.50
☐	7497 0139 0	**Snow Spider**	Jenny Nimmo	£2.50
☐	7497 0140 4	**Emlyn's Moon**	Jenny Nimmo	£2.25
☐	7497 0344 X	**The Haunting**	Margaret Mahy	£2.25
☐	416 96850 3	**Catalogue of the Universe**	Margaret Mahy	£1.95
☐	7497 0051 3	**My Friend Flicka**	Mary O'Hara	£2.99
☐	7497 0079 3	**Thunderhead**	Mary O'Hara	£2.99
☐	7497 0219 2	**Green Grass of Wyoming**	Mary O'Hara	£2.99
☐	416 13722 9	**Rival Games**	Michael Hardcastle	£1.99
☐	416 13212 X	**Mascot**	Michael Hardcastle	£1.99
☐	7497 0126 9	**Half a Team**	Michael Hardcastle	£1.99
☐	416 08812 0	**The Whipping Boy**	Sid Fleischman	£1.99
☐	7497 0033 5	**The Lives of Christopher Chant**	Diana Wynne-Jones	£2.50
☐	7497 0164 1	**A Visit to Folly Castle**	Nina Beachcroft	£2.25

All these books are available at your bookshop or newsagent, or can be ordered direct from the publisher. Just tick the titles you want and fill in the form below.

Mandarin Paperbacks, Cash Sales Department, PO Box 11, Falmouth, Cornwall TR10 9EN.

Please send cheque or postal order, no currency, for purchase price quoted and allow the following for postage and packing:

UK   80p for the first book, 20p for each additional book ordered to a maximum charge of £2.00.

BFPO   80p for the first book, 20p for each additional book.

Overseas   £1.50 for the first book, £1.00 for the second and 30p for each additional book
including Eire thereafter.

NAME (Block letters) ....

ADDRESS ....

....

....